## "You like your astronomy," Dominic observed

Mickey took a step a[...]
close that his breathi[...]
her back.

"It keeps things in perspective."

"Something like the 'you're just a grain of sand on
the beach of humanity' theory?"

"No," she replied. "There are constants and there
are subtle shifts that are always evolving. The universe
expands, time slows or increases, but it doesn't matter.
The rotation about the sun, the orbit of the moon—
those don't change. It's a great fusion of dynamic
and static forces all working together in concert."

He had no idea what she was talking about, but
he was willing to listen to her voice forever. Their
discussion didn't involve drugs or penny-ante larceny,
or even who was winning at the races. Her words were
the closest thing to a normal conversation he'd had in
two years of undercover work, and he realized how
much he missed it. "A philosopher as well as an
astronomer," he murmured.

"That's not philosophy—that's physics."

*"Who are you?"* he asked, no longer able to continue
with the game they were playing.

"Are you really sure you want to know?" She raised
her brows as she asked.

And he was a goner.

Dear Reader,

Okay, if you're a geek please raise your hand. Yes, I was a geek, too. It wasn't fun, mostly awkward and painful. However, all awkward and painful things must come to an end, and eventually I realized how lucky I was to be blessed with *geekiness*. As such, Mickey holds a special place in my heart because she's the heroine of THE BACHELORETTE PACT whose character is closest to my own. When I was creating the story, I knew I wanted to give her a special hero—a man living in a *different* world, but who was as isolated as she was in hers. And so Dominic flashed to mind, and instantly I was in love.

Next month is Beth's story, and do I ever have a surprise in store for you! But I won't spoil it...you'll just have to read to find out.

I love hearing from my readers. Please let me know what you think. Visit my Web site at www.kathleenoreilly.com or drop me a line at P.O. Box 312, Nyack, NY 10960.

*Kathleen O'Reilly*

## Books by Kathleen O'Reilly

**HARLEQUIN TEMPTATION**
889—JUST KISS ME
927—ONCE UPON A MATTRESS
*967—PILLOW TALK

**HARLEQUIN DUETS**
66—A CHRISTMAS CAROL

*The Bachelorette Pact

# KATHLEEN O'REILLY

## IT SHOULD HAPPEN TO YOU

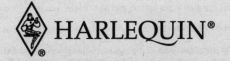

HARLEQUIN®

TORONTO • NEW YORK • LONDON
AMSTERDAM • PARIS • SYDNEY • HAMBURG
STOCKHOLM • ATHENS • TOKYO • MILAN • MADRID
PRAGUE • WARSAW • BUDAPEST • AUCKLAND

Special thanks to Jennifer Adelman-McCarthy
for her help with answering questions about astrophysics.
Any errors are entirely mine.

ISBN 0-373-69171-8

IT SHOULD HAPPEN TO YOU

Visit us at www.eHarlequin.com

**Printed in U.S.A.**

# 1

By ALL RIGHTS, it should have been a glorious day in Chicago. After all, it's not every day your best friend gets married. It's not every day that your maid of honor dress actually looks good and—as an even bigger bonus—fits you well enough that you might actually want to wear it again. Mickey Coleman forced a smile.

*It's not every day that you're videotaped having sex.*

She allowed herself one quick shudder. Oh, God. Oh, God. Oh, God. And that from a woman who was decidedly *not* religious.

She looked across the church's small dressing room where Jessica, in blissful ignorance, was adjusting her veil. Jessica, who'd never been videotaped having sex in her entire life.

Mickey spent all of two minutes debating whether to dump on her best friend on her wedding day. Eventually, guilt prevailed and she realized that not even Mickey the Idiot was that stupid.

"Anything wrong?" Beth asked, coming up beside her. "You look a little pale." Beth, sweet, innocent Beth, blinked her huge baby blues.

Mickey pulled off her glasses and wiped the lenses, as if that was the problem. "It's the dress. The color is a little off for me."

"I think it looks great on you."

Mickey's mouth twisted into a pale imitation of a smile. "Yeah, I do, too."

This stupid dress was more than half of the problem. They had Jessica's bachelorette party right after the last fitting. *Oh, Mickey, you should wear it out. You look fab!*

Mickey didn't wear dresses that showed more than the requisite one-third of her breasts. And she didn't normally drink more than four beers in one night. And she didn't normally have one-night stands with horny college interns who threaten blackmail.

The panic attack started all over again.

"Are you sure you're okay?" Beth asked.

"I think I just need to sit down." Mickey managed to choke the words out, and then collapsed onto a nearby folding chair.

"Want some water?"

"Yeah, that'll help. Thanks."

Beth came back with a paper cup and handed it over. "I know this has been hard for you."

Mickey stared in confusion. How did she know? "What?"

Beth tilted her head in Jessica's direction. "Jessica. Adam. The wedding. You know, you're not losing a best friend. You're gaining a whole new conduit to eligible bachelors."

The sad thing was, Beth was completely serious. "I hadn't thought of it that way," Mickey said, completely honest.

"I know we kinda made this bachelorette pact promise, but we were kidding, right?" Beth blinked hopefully.

The Bachelorette Pact. Almost twelve months ago the four college friends had made a promise to revel in their single status. Free of men, free to do whatever they wanted. Oh, yeah, paradise. Right now the free-of-men part sounded great, because today her priorities were getting the tape, of a night she didn't even remember—much. Then she could concentrate on the galaxy density differentiation presentation for Dr. Heidelman. Her ticket to fame and fortune in the scientific community. Well, not really fortune, but definitely fame among the Astrophysical Journal set. And maybe even respect in the eyes of one Dr. Andrew Coleman, MD, the man otherwise known as Dad. If Dad ever heard about that tape, or anyone at Astrophysical Sciences Research Center for that matter, she'd be pretty much astrophysical toast.

The day after the Bachelorette Party, John Monihan had approached her with vague references about their evening before. Apparently he was one of those video aficionados, just her luck. Now he had the tape of their night, and he wanted payback. Actually, he merely wanted more sex, which was very frustrating, because Mickey just didn't remember it being that great.

Beth pulled up a chair next to her. "You know, we can do stuff together, too. I mean, if you want to."

This time Mickey's smile was legit. Beth, at her most earnest, couldn't be denied. "Sure, Beth. Maybe we can go out after the reception."

"Brick's for a beer?"

Beer? Not in a million years. Still, there were always the uncharted waters of new territories, like, say, martinis. "Sure."

The music cranked up from the chapel, and the wedding planner rushed them out into the foyer. Mickey walked over to where Jessica was standing in front of the mirror, twisting around to see her back. When Jessica spied her, she gave Mickey one last hug.

"Break a leg," Mickey whispered.

"You'll be next," was all Jessica had to say.

Oh yeah, right. Slimeball antimatter was definitely prime husband material. Mickey held her tongue.

The ceremony was beautiful, she had to say that. White lilies, classical music and barely controlled tears that hung stubbornly at the corners of her eyes. When Adam kissed Jessica, Mickey nearly lost it.

Jessica smiled at her from under her veil, a tremulous smile completely ruined by the steely glint in her eyes that said, "You're catching the bouquet." That was Jessica. Always the woman in denial.

The exit music started, true love conquering all, a journey to a new life, yada, yada, yada.

Mickey sighed, grabbed the arm of the best man and followed the happy couple down the aisle and out the door. The best man smiled at her, a harmless, unpretentious smile, and Mickey just nodded curtly.

He was one of the enemy. He was a man, and right now she had little patience for human beings with an extra appendage. She'd been shot down by those flyboys one too many times.

"I bet you have a video camera," she whispered under her breath, a reminder that harmless, unpretentious smiles could hide the nefarious heart of a debauchee.

"As a matter of fact, I do," he said. "It's in the car. Should I bring it in?"

Mickey didn't answer, just gave him the patented Coleman growl, guaranteed to intimidate any man, woman or Department of Energy inspector. So was this a testosterone-laden man or merely an invertebrate munchkin? The age-old question reared its head.

He shot her one frightened look and that was the end of the conversation.

Mickey buffed her nails on the shoulder of the polished-silk dress. The man was nothing more than Milquetoast in a tux.

WHILE CASSANDRA DECORATED the getaway car with all sorts of suggestions and advice for every newly wedded couple, Mickey supervised. Eventually the wedding party—sans bride and groom, who were probably off doing the rumpy-pumpy—had managed to completely eliminate any possibility of driver-side visibility.

All in all, it was great bawdy fun.

But all good things must come to an end. The reception was winding down, the sun was starting to set, and finally the happy couple appeared, a telltale flush in Jessica's cheeks. Sex had definitely been involved. Jess threw the bouquet at Mickey, who dodged and bobbed. In accordance with Murphy's laws on weddings and other damned affairs, the thing hit her smack on the chest.

Using lightning-fast reflexes, which she'd never before possessed, she tossed it off to Beth.

Eventually Jessica's Porsche pulled away from the curb. Mickey waved goodbye, wiping away her tears before anyone noticed. Her best friend was married. So why couldn't she be happier for her?

It wasn't as if she wished divorce or death on Adam; she just wished that things wouldn't change. But already she'd noticed the little differences. Jessica tried hard, but she was becoming a clock-watcher when they went out. And worse, only once had she participated in Cassandra's favorite sport, the ten-thousand meter, manly-man ogle. To top it off, she compared the subject in question to Adam—favoring Adam, of course.

It was all depressing.

In order to dispel some of her depression, and forget the whole tape-sex-blackmail-I-have-shot-my-career-to-hell debacle, she met up with Beth and Cassandra at Brick's that evening.

Saturday nights were always packed, full of males and females on the make. Mickey traded in breast cleavage and heels for her favorite blue jeans and Polymorph T-shirt. Much safer.

Cassandra, spiffily attired in a fire-engine red sheath that revealed every single one of her Pilates-honed curves, shook her head. "Cinderella's regressed back to rags."

"Yeah, fairy tale's over. Reality bites."

Sometimes it was rough having an overabundance of brains and an underabundance of whatever it was that guys liked, she thought to herself. Everywhere she looked, the male eyes in the bar were glued to Cassandra's parts.

A short time later two men in suits came over and began chatting with Cassandra and Beth, and Mickey wondered cynically who wore a suit on Saturday. Beth eventually broke free of the lesser suit and joined

Mickey in the girls-gone-solo club, ordering chips and salsa for them both.

Beth fished in the basket for the biggest chip and wistfully studied it, shifting the golden triangle in the light. "It's three points, but I've been starving myself all week. Tonight's a celebration."

"Oh, boy," replied Mickey glumly, punching her chip in the picante. "Why'd you leave the potential life mate?"

"Too much cologne."

"Yeah, I hate that," Mickey replied, a little bit of snide in her tone, which covered the fact that she was envious as hell. Beth had never achieved envy-worthy status before. Out of all of them, Cassandra had the hot luck with the guys. Jess had the great family that understood how families were supposed to be. And now, she had the great new husband. As for Beth, Mickey had never spent much time being jealous of Beth.

Until now.

She crunched the chip with more force than necessary, a strong bite of jalapeño making her eyes water. Spitefully she swallowed the demon vegetable whole.

Mickey Coleman Cushing—jalapeño eater extraordinaire. Now there's a talent.

She sighed. Now, see, this was the main problem with having a large ego. The falls from grace were light-years to the ground.

Covertly she studied Beth, who wasn't as sexy as Cassandra, wasn't as ambitious as Jessica, and wasn't as smart as Mickey. Beth, who was completely happy with who she was.

"How do you manage to be so content with who you are?" asked Mickey.

Beth just grimaced. "I know you don't think much of me..."

There were times Mickey didn't think much of anyone; that's what made her world such a lonely place. "That's not true," she said automatically, then popped a chip into her mouth.

"No, it's okay. I know what you think and you're wrong."

Mickey stopped and swallowed, now more than slightly curious. "What do I think?"

"That I'm a weaker female destined to dilute the genetic line of females everywhere because I believe that man is necessary for the betterment of the species."

It really did sound like something she would say. When had she gotten so bitter? Oh, yeah, she'd been born that way. "No, that's not true. Exactly."

"I think now is a good time for me to learn from you. You're so focused and independent. You have your life together, and I feel so...needy. Maybe if we hang together, some of you will rub off on me? That is, if you want to."

And here was Mickey, feeling all smug and superior, when her life was lower than a Jerry Springer show. She was being blackmailed. Because of sex. Sex which she hardly ever had. Oh, the irony. "If only you knew," Mickey murmured.

"Knew what?" Beth asked, sipping at her wine.

"That focused, independent people whose lives are so together make some of the most nuclear mistakes in the world."

"No!" Beth exclaimed, and such emphatic disbelief was almost refreshing. As if Mickey was not capable of mental burps. "What kind of mistakes?"

Now came the hard part. Admitting that she—who really considered her only true quality to be her brain—could do something so stupid. "Remember the bachelorette party the other night?"

Beth nodded.

"Remember how I disappeared?"

Again, the head nod.

Mickey took a long drink of alcohol. Even one-hundred proof couldn't numb the embarrassment. "I can't do this."

Sensing imminent meltdown, Beth waved her hand. "Yes, yes, you can."

Perhaps Mickey should keep her mouth shut. But she'd spent so much of her life needing to angst that silence was impossible. "Oh, all right. I've got to tell somebody. After I left the bar, I called up John, this intern at work—he looks all of thirteen—and asked if I could come over."

"He's not really thirteen, is he? I can see the headlines. *Statutory Seduction: Physicist Charged In Boy-Toy Scandal.*"

Mickey coughed as a straight shot of gin came back up her nose. "Oh, yes, that would look good. Thankfully, no, he's a senior in college. But still..."

Beth nodded. "You know, that's really very sexy right now. May, December. Woman in the dominant position. That's not so bad."

No, that wasn't the bad part. Mickey took another

long, brain-cell-killing dreg of the martini. "He video-taped me. Him. You know, when we were..."

There was no condemnation in Beth's eyes, only a glow of admiration. "No joke? That's so adventurous of you. I thought only Cassandra went down the red-light path."

Adventurous? Yeah, that was one way of looking at it. "I didn't know." Mickey took another long drink. "Now he wants to do it again."

Beth twirled her chip in the bowl of salsa, as if reading the future in the onions and tomatoes. "The taping or the sex?"

"The sex."

"Just like Pamela Sue..." Then Beth looked up, and her eyes got huge. "Oh...and if you don't, he's going to put you on the Internet. Oh, man, I hope you don't look fat."

Mickey, who had never considered the fat aspect, shuddered in horror. "I've got an article to finish. I'm working the presentation for Heidelman. I'll be the punch line in every joke for the next decade, playing into every stereotype that exists for the little woman." She rammed her fist on the table, very un-little woman. "I've got to get that tape back."

"Can you buy it from him?"

"No. I already offered. Stupid jerk." She'd covered all possible aspects in order to salvage her career. Extortion, bribery, excessive pleading and murder. There was only one solution left. "I think I'm going to steal it," she announced. It seemed better to state it confidently, as if she thought this could actually work.

"You could get caught," replied Beth, pointing out the one elephantine flaw.

However, Mickey had already considered that. "That's why I need a professional." *So Mickey wouldn't get caught.*

"A private detective?"

Mickey glanced around, checking to make sure no big ears were listening. "Nah. I mean a professional criminal. You know, a real thief. Unfortunately, now I've got to find somebody. You don't meet many criminals in the lab."

"I know just the man," said Beth, quick as you please.

Amazed, Mickey stared at her with new appreciation. "You really know criminals?"

Beth lifted one eyebrow. "You meet people from all walks of life in a Starbucks. Come in tomorrow about ten. He hangs out at a table near the coffee-mug-clearance shelf in the back."

Mickey considered it for a moment. It was so tempting. "What do you think he's into? Drugs?"

Beth shook her head. "I don't think so. I think he's a made guy."

Huh? The foreign terminology made Mickey wonder at the sheltered life she had led. "What's that?" she asked.

"Part of the Outfit."

Her jaw dropped open. "No way. A mafia guy?"

Beth preened. "Yup. Right in my own Starbucks. Venti latte. Loaded."

Starbucks. It was a long way from *The Godfather*. Times had changed.

Mickey took another sip of the martini. The alcohol

was beginning to make everything seem logical. "How do you know that he's one of Them?"

"I saw his driver's license once when he flipped open his wallet. Dominic Corlucci."

Mickey still wasn't convinced. "Just because he has an Italian name doesn't mean anything."

"Trust me, Mickey. A woman gets a sense about these things."

A scientist would be laughed out of the lab on hunches and womanly instincts, but Beth sounded so sure, even in the absence of any conclusive evidence. Mickey thought instincts ranked right up there with the tooth fairy, and could rationalize the whole thing away with logic and science when she wanted to. *That* she had inherited from her father.

It all sounded glamorous and possibly real. The Mafia. She took another sip of her drink. She'd always had a major thing for Pacino.

Still, the Mafia.

It wasn't exactly what she had planned. She'd been thinking of one of those penny-ante types that wore pants that were too short and hung out at the racetrack. In the end, did she really have a choice?

It was her career on the line. Her reputation as a professional and as an astronomer. No way were they going to take away her stars.

The mob ate guys like Monihan for dinner. That made her smile. It'd definitely be worth it. And worst case, she would lay even odds that the Witness Protection Program didn't have one astrophysicist in their ranks.

*Yet.*

"BETH. PSSSSSSSTTT. BETH."

Beth stared blankly, her face half-hidden by a cappuccino machine.

Oh, this was good. No recognition at all. The disguise was working. She'd had to leave her glasses on, because she was blind without them. Not that it seemed to affect the whole look. Mickey disguised as a bimbo had been a masterstroke. Who would suspect?

Mickey placed a hand on her hip, forming a nice isosceles triangle, just as she'd seen the other girls do.

"May I help you?" Beth asked.

"It's Mickey," she answered, twitching a little because the spandex skirt was hitting her butt in all the wrong places.

Beth emerged from behind the cappuccino machine and started to smile. "It's always been a big, fat lie, hasn't it?"

"What?"

"The whole 'I hate men' thing. Look at you," she said, her hand encompassing spandex, lace and thigh-high boots. "You just jumped from the latest issue of Sluts R Us."

Not exactly the look Mickey had been trying for. "Are you trying to make me feel better?"

Beth finished up the coffee she'd been making and put it on the wooden bar. "I'm not, huh?"

Mickey shook her head.

Beth grinned. "Well, girlfriend, you're going to be fighting the vice cops off with a stick."

When Beth started thinking she was witty, they were in serious trouble. "Where is he?"

Beth cocked her head in the direction of the far corner. "That's his usual table. He's not here yet."

"Okay." Mickey, who'd secretly been looking forward to mingling with the wrong kind, felt a little disappointed.

She practiced her walk over to the small round table. Hip to the right, hip to the left, thrust, thrust, thrust. There was a certain samba feel to it, not that Mickey had ever danced the samba, but if she had, it would have given her that same all-over body tingle that she had now.

Three espressos later, he walked through the door. Instantly she knew who he was. He moved with a sleek, lean grace, no squeaky tennies here. The kind of man who could kill you before you even knew he was in the room. His shoulders were broad, probably from lifting bodies. All in all, he was one dangerous hombre.

What scared Mickey was that, although Beth had told her enough that she would be able to recognize him, Beth had failed to disclose how a woman's body would react. A logical, intelligent, rational woman's body.

Mickey sat up straighter in her seat. Her back, her chin, her breasts all snapping into place. She'd taken a course in body language, she knew what she was saying.

*Come on, baby, light my fire* was the same in all languages.

Cold dark eyes scanned the room, settling on her.

*Uh-oh.*

The room temperature dropped ten degrees. In that moment, it dawned on her this was a really *stupid* idea.

He was going to kill her. He had the look of a man

who carried a tommy gun in his pocket, or even worse, a garrote. Automatically, her hand covered her throat.

The next thing she knew, this cold-blooded killer was looming over her table. "You got three seconds to move your pretty little ass clear of my table."

*My table.* Her eyes narrowed. Nothing like arrogance to piss a woman off, especially Mickey. She had heard the tone before. Dr. Breedlove had tried it her rookie year at Astrophysical Sciences Research Center. Her nuclei and elementary particles prof at U of C tried it, too, and both had been easily shot down. That's what happened when you could solve Maxwell's equation at the age of eighteen.

Mickey pulled at her tortoiseshell glasses until she could stare down her nose at him. "I'm here on business, so you might as well stop your gawking and sit your pretty little ass right down." She smiled innocently. "Sweet cheeks."

The coolness in the dark eyes heated. Damn, he was a handsome devil. Handsome in the ways of those Italian boys with high cheekbones and dark, brooding looks that said, "Casanova was my grandfather."

Not the sort of man that roamed the composite-floor hallways at Astrophysical Sciences Research Center.

Not that she was noticing, or anything. Defiantly she raised her chin.

"Say what you want to say. It's a free country." Then he sprawled into the tiny chair next to her, his legs comfortably apart. A pose designed to draw attention to his well-muscled thighs and his well-muscled other parts.

Not that she was noticing, or anything.

Mickey tore her gaze away from his parts. "I want to hire you."

His reaction wasn't quite what she wanted. His legs closed, his arms folded across his chest, and his eyes could've turned her to stone. "No."

"You haven't even asked what I want you to do."

He stared up at the ceiling, doing a fine job of avoiding her eyes. "I don't want to know."

This was not good. "I could pay you," she whispered. "Pay you well." The dark eyes flickered back to earth.

"I don't do anything illegal," he said, slow and quiet, in a tone that implied that he did things illegal on a daily basis.

Mickey took a sip of coffee. "It's not that illegal. I've got some property that needs returning."

"To who?" he asked.

"Whom," she corrected, now portraying the part of a bimbo grammarian. *Focus, Mick.* "To me."

"You got the wrong city block for drug deals gone bad."

"No drugs. It's a tape."

His dark eyebrows drew together at a perfect forty-five degree angle. "Who's holding it?"

Mickey slid a piece of paper across the table. Slimeball Intern's name and address were printed in twelve-point Arial type so that there were no mistakes. She'd seen that on *Law & Order.*

"How much are we talking here?"

"Two-hundred dollars."

The eyes closed off again. "Sorry, lady."

Quickly Mickey backtracked. The going rate for breaking and entering was not posted on CNN. "Two thousand." It would kill her savings, but for a career-sustaining insurance policy, it was worth it. She needed muscle, and she was willing to pay for it.

Again she caught the flicker of interest in his face before it disappeared. "No."

"Please," she said. It was about the closest she'd ever come to begging in her entire life, but she needed help.

"How do you know there's only one tape?"

Mickey closed her eyes. This was where things got tricky and moved into the realm of diplomatic finagling. "If there's more than one tape, then work—of a more forceful nature—might be involved. You do any leg breaking? Whacking?" she asked, successfully imagining Slimeball Intern screaming in pain. She smiled.

"No," he said, and the screams in her dreams drifted away.

"Oh," she muttered softly, thinking it was probably a good thing that Slimeball Intern wouldn't get hurt. Secretly she was still disappointed.

"So you'll do it?" she asked, just as the door swung open. The bells on the top jangled, and a big man walked through. Big, beefy, with frown lines that were carved permanently into his face.

Mickey shot a quick glance in Beth's direction to see if she'd been watching, but right now Beth was missing. And where was moral support when you needed it? Off refilling the Frappuccino mix.

Slowly the big guy lumbered over to where she was sitting.

"We're done," Dominic said to Mickey, as if she were nothing more than a nanofly.

Sensing the other man was a business associate, in the

haziest definition of the word, Mickey stood. "You'll do it?"

He didn't reply, just grabbed her and dumped her in his lap.

*Whoa.*

"What—"

And he kissed her. Oh, God. Oh, God. Oh, God...

An electrical charge fired everywhere he touched, and somewhere in her nether regions condensation began to form. What had she been missing out on by not kissing wise guys before? That was the last thing she remembered before her brain began to spark and fizzle.

Her body melted, draping over his in a nicely accommodating fashion. Another two nanoseconds and she'd be ready for sex.

He stopped before she really embarrassed herself, which was a good thing. Then he patted her bum and whispered in her ear, "You need to get out of here really, really fast. Meet me here tomorrow at ten. I'll help you, but don't say anything right now."

Like she was capable of speech. *Ha.*

For a long moment she stared at him, trying to read exactly what he was thinking. This time what she saw in his eyes surprised her. None of the "leg-breaking" coldness, nor the "Come to me, *cara mia*" heat, but instead there was just—curiosity. The kind that she saw everyday at Astrophysical Sciences Research Center.

She blinked, and whoosh—it was gone and the cold was back.

"See you later," he said, in a husky tone that implied all sorts of carnal treats. He spoiled it all by giving her another pat on the rear.

She should have socked him, but that "later" part was still echoing in her head.

Then she glanced at the big Gonzo that cast a long shadow over the table. "Yeah, all right," she said, then pulled down her glasses, just so he didn't think he could boss her around. "Sweet cheeks."

# 2

DOMINIC CORLUCCI HAD to work hard to keep the smile off his face. A woman like that? She could make a man forget a lot.

However, Dominic's memories were too well ingrained to forget anything. Self-preservation was his number-one priority now. The only reason he had kissed her was to stave off unnecessary questions; his companion saw one use in a woman and one use only.

Maybe that was his only reason, or maybe she aroused his curiosity—among other things.

He watched her walk away, an exaggerated swing in her hips that didn't look normal. He didn't know who she was, but he did know that something reeked of a setup. That worried him.

"So I was telling Louise, 'Louise,' I said, 'I'm not ready to settle down. If you're looking for a man to play house with, then you need to be finding greener pastures.'"

Dom turned his attention away from the puzzle of the retreating female and back to the job at hand. Namely Frankie "Lumpy" DeCarlo.

"Yeah, females ain't nothing but trouble," he muttered, trying to figure her angle.

"Amen. Who's the legs?"

"A potential sheet warmer. Need to try her on for size." He cracked his knuckles for effect.

The big man considered it for a moment, rubbing his chin. "I'd do her."

Dom stretched in the damned little seat, all casual, a man having a cup of coffee, nothing more. "You seen her around before?"

Frankie scratched his head. "You know, she looks a little like Big Jake's ex, but that one—and she was trouble, I tell you—didn't wear no glasses. Odd look, the glasses and all."

Definitely odd. Dom didn't trust anybody. A man got real dead, real fast that way. "Yeah, but it's kinda cute, don't you think?"

"Me, I like my women stacked. A man needs something to hold on to."

Dom gave Frankie a sideways look. "I bet you have all the women panting after you."

Frankie gave him a palms-up. "All my problems can be attributed to slow horses and fast women. I'm a veritable babe in the woods compared to you lothario types."

Dom kept silent. It helped his image when he didn't talk about women; he just smiled mysteriously every now and then. Made everybody wonder. He smiled now, the smile of a man remembering his last good lay.

"I haven't seen Johnny C. around lately," he said, casually changing the subject. "Where's he gone? Sold us out for those guys back east?"

"Don't know. Vinny's been keeping quiet lately." Frankie looked around, watching the other people in the store. "Let's go to Dilly's place."

Dilly's place was a good sign. Dom hadn't yet been invited to the more sacrosanct confines, and if he was getting an invitation now, that meant Frankie was starting to trust him.

That might be the perfect time to pitch his ATM scam. Nothing obvious or too eager. Cast the floater out and then just skim the line back and forth over the surface.

Dom uncurled his legs and stood. That was the bitch of these little places. A tall man needed a place to stretch out.

He caught the eye of the street cop that walked in the door. Badge 271. They'd been in the Academy together. Dom shrugged into his jacket, keeping his face turned away. The cops didn't worry him as much as the attorneys. Cops knew to keep their mouths shut. But an attorney? Slimeballs who were paid to yap. Still, as he walked past 271, he kept his face firmly in the shadows. Big Frankie didn't notice at all.

MICKEY CAUGHT HER reflection in the rearview mirror, just as she hit the highway to Batavia. She had forgotten to rub off her eyeliner. Not that anyone would notice. Nobody really noticed her looks except when she was dolled up, either as a bridesmaid, or a bimbo.

Neither of which was her.

No, guys like Dominic Corlucci would never notice Mickey in the world that she lived in.

He was the polar opposite of Slimeball Intern Monihan and a hell of a kisser. Her lips were still tingling from the effects, and if she closed her eyes she could still recall the centrifugal force that was buzzing between her legs.

Times like this, a woman could be glad that the man was a gangster. It made him oh so easy to resist.

Definitely trouble. In fact, by the time she'd made it to the triple-axe sculpture that bridged high over the entrance to the lab, she had made up her mind. No point in endangering her loins or her life. She could just forget about Dominic Corlucci altogether.

*I'm not going to be disappointed about it, either,* she thought sternly to herself and to all body parts that reverberated whenever his magnetic field snapped its fingers.

She slid her badge into the front-door locks and went inside the long narrow corridors. Astrophysical Sciences Research Center. This was her home. Sometimes it still overwhelmed her. Quarks, tau neutrino, hell, even the Internet was conceived of here, contrary to what the politicians thought. These were the discoveries that rocked the world.

These discoveries were the very building blocks of the universe. People never appreciated the simplicity of the atom and all its components. Such a small, simple body, so powerful yet so overlooked.

And Mickey knew just how that felt.

Her sneakers squeaked as she walked down the halls where Lederman had walked. The seventh floor of the high-rise was where she did her work, and she found her way to the small, functional desk in the back of the pen.

She worked on the Sloan Digital Sky Survey, which she considered her own personal heaven. Mapping out the cosmos with pictures and light. That was all Mickey had ever wanted to do—work with the stars.

Every morning the schedule was the same, even if

she came in late, which she was today. The great thing about research was that most scientists kept odd hours. Inspiration couldn't be scheduled, nor could experiments that took three years to complete.

She turned on her computer and checked e-mail first. Empty. Next, just because she was a creature of habit, she checked to see who was online.

Chao: Unavailable.

Dr. Lindstrom: Available.

J.: Unavailable.

Yeah, Jessica was off having a honeymoon in China. Dejected, Mickey rolled back in her chair. Mountain climbing, which was about the silliest thing that Mickey had ever heard. Her ideal honeymoon would involve a trip to Geneva to see CERN and possibly some sightseeing. Then a long week in the hotel, with room service and HBO.

In lieu of actually having someone to talk to, Mickey started typing to herself.

*"M, what's up?"*

She clicked Send and delighted herself when new mail appeared. Getting into the game, she hit Reply and started typing.

*"M, glad you asked. What to do, what to do? I'm not a girlie-girl. I don't want to be a girlie-girl. But I keep doing these stupid men things. Just like a girlie-girl. Does that make me an idiot?"*

Then she clicked Send.

Magically, a few moments later, she had new mail. She started hammering away at the keyboard.

*"M, no, you're not a girlie-girl, because all members of the Coleman family—except your mother, and we're not going to*

*talk about that—are scientists. We use our brains to succeed where others have failed."*

Send.

*"If I'm not a failure, then why am I being blackmailed with a sex tape? Why am I considering an affiliation with the mob? Why am I attracted to Dominic?"*

Send.

*"M, I lied. You're a loser AND a girlie-girl. Get over it."*

Mickey stared at her screen and wished that the J-woman was back. Jessica wasn't this harsh.

Maybe she should build Beth a computer and teach her how to use it. Actually, that wasn't a bad idea. To-morrow, definitely tomorrow.

She took a quick look up to the front of the bull pen.

Damn, John was in. His Michael Crichton *Sphere* screen saver flickered eerily in the fluorescent lighting. *Of course* he couldn't be sick today. Illness would be nice. Something vile and long lasting with symptoms that included pain-racked stomach spasms, huge bouts of nausea and perhaps a high fever, where he might be so incapacitated that he would simply hand over the tape.

She'd seen that on TV once.

When he walked into the room ten minutes later, he looked disgustingly healthy. Now, when she looked at him, her poor vision free of lust and alcohol, she could see the weak chin, the beady eyes that darted like a rat's. Man, she had been so blind before. It was proba-bly his golden hair that had blinded her to the rest of his faults. Yeah, definitely. The laughing blue eyes—that darted like a rat's, of course—hadn't helped.

Then he winked at her. Winked. As if she would be

happy to see him. He was lucky she wasn't working in the Tevatron. Proton collisions could be really messy. One false move, and zap—a human body could be transported to—well, everywhere, really. Just tiny Monihan particles floating in the air. Wouldn't that be nice?

Oblivious to her degenerative thoughts, he lifted his Coke in greeting and strolled over. "Top of the morning, Miss Coleman. We on for this evening?"

She stared down at him over her glasses. "Go choke on a quark, Monihan."

"I love it when you get feisty." He pitched his voice an octave higher, "Oh, baby, yeah, right there..."

Had she really said that? Thank God she'd been too drunk to remember. She kept her eyes on her computer screen and whispered. "I got friends, Monihan. Friends that can really hurt you. I wouldn't be so quick to make jokes."

He leaned forward, the laughing blue eyes deadly serious. "You think this a joke? Not at all. Your career's been shot into a black hole unless you cooperate. You know the presentation for Heidelman? I'll bring the video."

"I could go to Heidelman and just report you for sexual harassment."

He looked intrigued. "Are you going to? A tough character-defining choice. Which is more important to you? Justice or your academic image? That's how you know what you're really made of. Which path are you going to take?"

Mickey looked up, close enough where she could see the true ugliness of his nature. "What has happened to you? You used to be nice, now you're just a bastard. Have you ever seen what a positron beam can do to human flesh? I'd say that's one directional splatter we've yet to map. What do you say, John? Want to go down in history?''

He took a sip of cola, looking completely unfazed by threats of evaporation. ''Does that mean we're on for tonight? I've got to work late in the lab this evening, but for you? I'll wait up.''

Wait up? He'd have to wait for hell to freeze, for time travel to be possible and for the discovery of Higgs Boson. ''I have a hot date with my boyfriend,'' she said.

''You don't have a boyfriend, Mickey. Remember?''

She raised an eyebrow. Very Queen Elizabeth. ''Maybe I do.''

''Yeah, right. Look, I'll let you have your fun. Tonight you're off the hook. And I'll be nice and leave you the weekend free, but come Monday...'' His voice trailed off, and he flicked a finger under her chin.

At his touch, she flinched, saddened that she'd actually had a pleasant carnal-knowledge experience with this creep. ''You're watching too many bad movies, Monihan.''

He walked over to his computer and clicked on his mouse a few times. Instantly the air was filled with moans and heavy breathing.

She slapped her hand down on her desk, welcoming the pain. ''Shut it off.''

''Monday night?''

When the seventh quark was discovered, and not a moment before. Mickey shot him a dire look. ''Whatever.''

IT WAS DARK OUT; the apartment complex was in a seedy part of the South Side. Thankfully, security lights were nonexistent. Mickey brought out her flashlight as they made their way to the side of the building.

"Ready?" she asked, whispering behind her.

"Are you sure we should be doing this?" was Beth's sole vote of confidence.

"I don't have a choice."

"Yeah, you do. Hire Dominic."

"He's too expensive. And besides that, he's dangerous."

"Well, yes. But expensive means that he's good, and you live for danger."

Mickey shone her flashlight in Beth's face to see if she was serious. Not a trace of a smile. Sometimes Beth scared her.

"I can do this," Mickey answered, just as she found the old fire escape. Bingo.

"And why do you think that?"

Mickey pulled at the ladder, and the whole world resounded with the painful creak. "I researched breaking and entering on the Internet."

Behind her, she heard the sound of Beth rolling her eyeballs.

Now wasn't the time for naysayers, though. She searched through her bag until she found the can of WD-40. *There's always another use.* Little did the advertisers realize, it could also be used for B and E. One spritz and the ladder was as quiet as the lab on Sunday.

"Okay, Shifty, what do we do next?" asked Beth.

Mickey climbed onto the fire escape and got to the second floor. Quickly Beth scampered up behind her.

Then Mickey shone her light on the wooden window frame. It looked just like the diagram on the Net. "We can lift up on this and slide it off its tracks."

"I'll take this side," said Beth, positioning herself at one end.

Mickey put down the flashlight and grabbed the other side. "One, two, three. Lift."

They heaved.

Nothing.

Mickey took a long breath. "Okay, we're just not putting enough into this."

"Excuse me. I was. I put everything into that lift. Aren't you supposed to know how to do this? Can we just teleport it, or something?"

"Transport. And that only works in *Star Trek*."

"I'm losing faith in you, Mickey. I didn't think this was going to work, but I told myself, 'No, if anybody can hypothesize her way out of this, it's you.' I was wrong." Beth, when tired, got mouthy.

Mickey, who had no patience for tired, mouthy women, shot her a warning look. "Shh. One more time."

They got in place again.

"One, two, three. Lift."

Somewhere in the dark they heard a noise.

"What was that?" Mickey asked, her heart pounding wildly.

Beth looked down below. "A cat."

"One more time."

"Maybe we could just break it?"

Mickey cased the joint, considering the idea. Everything was too quiet. "Nah. Somebody might hear us."

"Can we try the front door? Maybe it's unlocked."

"You have no imagination."

"Logic, Mick. It's called logic."

Beth had a point. Mickey abandoned her short life of crime. "Okay."

They climbed back down and entered the building's lobby. John's apartment was on the second floor, right at the top of the stairs. Mickey handed the flashlight to Beth and tried the doorknob.

Locked.

Beth stared at Mickey's hand, her mouth open. "You're wearing gloves?"

"I didn't want to leave any prints."

"And what about me?"

Mickey had researched that, too. "Your prints aren't on file. No worries."

"What? You've been arrested before?"

"No. Anybody that handles plutonium gets printed and filed in the national database. Procedure."

Beth got a little wide-eyed. "You really work with plutonium?"

"Nah. Just a little prison humor."

Beth wasn't amused. "Can we go now?"

A long beam of headlights lit up the window off the stairwell.

"Somebody's coming," Mickey said, and then took off up the stairs to the third floor. "Up here. If it's John, he won't see us."

Beth followed right behind, a streak in black spandex and sweater. Very stylish. Silently they waited for the door to open below.

The door eased open and an old man creaked his way

into the foyer. Mickey began to breathe again. "False alarm."

"Look, this isn't working. You need to hire Dominic."

Oh, hell.

Mickey leaned against the rickety stair rail and faced the whole truth. Sadly, her life as she knew it was pretty much screwed unless she got that tape back, and Dominic Corlucci, mob guy extraordinaire, seemed the best answer.

Somewhere upstairs, a stereo cranked up. Loud, discordant and really, really bad music.

Mickey sighed. "Oh, all right."

"Want to get a beer?"

"Soft drink for me," she answered. She was still paying for the aftereffects of her last binge.

"I'll buy."

Mickey stuffed her gloves in her pocket and studied her own attire. Black sweatshirt and matching knit pants. Passable, but barely. "You think we should change?"

Beth shook her head. "Nah. Black is very in."

# 3

ON SATURDAY MORNING, Mickey donned the long blond wig. She pulled the boots from her closet and searched for something remotely sleazy.

Nothing. Absolutely nothing. In disgust, she slapped her hand against the hard wooden frame and immediately regretted it. Swift, Coleman, very swift. She was going to have to do something about her wardrobe if she wanted to continue her disguise in front of Dominic Corlucci—which she did. Her alter ego was going to need some more clothes. She should talk to Cassandra about that. If there was one woman who knew sleaze— a tasteful sort of sleaze—it was Cassandra.

Dejected, she leaned against the closet frame. There was only one reason for this loss of steely self-control. Sex.

And one way to fix it. *Never again was she going to have sex.*

If Queen Victoria could do it, so could Mickey. Some little particle of double circled inside her, due mainly to the nighttime sightings of Dominic Corlucci in her dreams. Dreams that were starting to impact her sleeping abilities. But what harm was there in a little idle fantasizing? Mickey had always had a healthy fantasy life. And fantasies were allowed under the steely self-control regime. It kept the lonely Saturday nights interesting.

She shoved off the doubts and started strategizing her dress code, the pragmatic Mickey returning. If Dominic ever knew the real Mickey Coleman, he wouldn't give her the time of day, much less an interesting Saturday night, so fantasies were all she had.

Another hour later and she was at Beth's Starbucks in full regalia—creatively inspired by a *Victoria's Secret* catalog and utilizing underwear in a manner for which it was not intended. The black camisole turned heads, which she hoped was a good thing.

She ordered a latte and then settled herself at his table. Prepared for all eventualities, she pulled out the latest issue of *Scientific American*—discreetly tucked inside a *Playgirl*—and sat back to read.

Half an hour later, he showed. When he walked through the door, she experienced that extreme tickling inside her that seemed so odd. Again. What was it about him? Was it the long, lean body that moved so gracefully? Was it the hooded eyes that seemed as deep and dark as the blackest night sky? Whatever it was, it was powerful and scared the smegaroo right out of her. Mickey didn't like men to have power over her. She was arrogant enough to think she could make her way to the top on her own merits. Everything would have been fine except for John Monihan. Except for Dominic Corlucci. Maybe she was just doomed to be stupid with men.

Oh, enough already. She took one last confidence-building sip of her coffee and then stood, electing to operate from a position of dominance. "You're late."

His eyes flickered with amusement. "If I had known you were so...anxious, I'd have come sooner." He glanced over at the *Playgirl* and raised an eyebrow. "A little light reading?"

"For the articles only," she said, and then winced when she noticed the front page, Seven Sensational Positions to Achieve the Ultimate O. She shrugged a shoulder, feigning nonchalance. "We have a deal?"

He crossed his powerful arms over his chest, his T-shirt clinging to muscles that made her mouth salivate in a purely Pavlovian response. "Yeah, but there's one little thing I need."

At this point, Mickey would have promised him anything. "What?"

"I need an escort. Somebody to fill in for a while."

Anything except that. "Let me think about it for a minute. No."

Then he shrugged a shoulder, nothing nonchalant about it at all. "The deal's off."

A lesser woman would have stamped her foot. Mickey merely adjusted her glasses. "You're willing to walk away from two-thousand dollars because I won't decorate your arm?"

Evenly he met her eyes. "Yeah."

She pulled herself up to her full five feet eleven inches and stared down her nose. He was taller than her by half a head, but the effect was still good. "What kind of wise guy are you?"

And she had him. His eyes flickered, not a big move, but she caught it. His gaze slid over her, a look she was learning to recognize, guaranteed to drop her stomach three megaohms. Then he slowly shook his head, regret marking his expression. "All right. We do it your way."

She didn't feel like woman triumphant, only woman stupid, but determinedly she carried on. "It's a business transaction, Mr. Corlucci. I'll pay a quarter of your fee up front, a quarter after the first visit to Monihan's apartment and the remainder upon delivery of the tape."

"Very professional," he said with a smile.

"It's a job. Nothing more," she answered.

"Certainly Ms...? You never gave me your name."

"Jones. Foxy Jones."

His lips quirked. Okay, so it was a sham name, but he didn't have to think it was funny. "Can I call you Foxy, or should I just stick to Ms. Jones?"

"Use whatever moniker you choose. When can you get the tape?"

"Not tonight. I have a wedding tonight."

"A wedding?" How oddly domestic. Still, Italian-Americans were very family oriented, so maybe it was cultural rather than some subliminal yearning to find his life mate.

"I need a date...Foxy," he said coaxingly, his voice silky as sin.

Her heart tripped right over itself in its hurry to pump blood into her nether regions. "Oh, behave," she said, as much to her heart as to him.

"I'm being honest. Anthony Testa's youngest son is getting married. I was invited. Black-tie."

"No, I mean don't call me Foxy."

"I thought that was your name?"

"It's a nickname. Call me...Michelle." Very few people knew that Michelle was her real name. Her father had insisted on calling her Mickey—after Mickey Mantle. He said that her mother liked the way Michelle had sounded. Fragile and feminine and silly. Everything that Mickey abhorred.

"Michelle," he said, his mouth lingering on the first part and then drawing out the rest, making it sound fragile and feminine and...completely not silly.

"Don't wear it out," she snapped. "So, can you get the tape tonight?"

"Will your...friend be home this evening?"

Mickey didn't want to know John's schedule; she didn't want to think about knowing John's schedule. Now he just made her skin crawl. "How the hell should I know?"

"Do you know of a time when he's usually out? It'll make my job easier."

"During the day, Monday through Friday. He works business hours."

"So he's at home at night? Looks like I'm off the hook tonight, then. You can come with me to the wedding, can't you? Not a business deal, a date."

She had to try one last time. When Dominic Corlucci looked at her, he scared her, and not because she thought he would stuff her into a trunk. Her fears were deeper. Her sensible, logical, rational nature was careening out of control. Her father would never approve. She slammed that door shut, the noise reverberating in her brain. "I don't do 'black-tie.'"

"I'll knock five-hundred dollars off my fee. Forget the up-front payment. Go buy something..." his gaze moved up and down, over thighs, breasts, arms and legs "...nice."

She fought the urge to cover herself. *Think bimbo.* "Only pretend," she said, the best warning she could muster.

He looked offended, the dark eyes holding secrets that no man should know. "Your choice."

She nodded briskly. "Don't forget it."

"Should I pick you up at your apartment?"

"No!" God forbid he should know where she lived. Or what her name was. Or her real bra size. "I'll meet you at the corner of Canal and Jackson, in front of Union Station."

"Okay. Be there at five-thirty. I've got to buy a wedding present."

A wedding present? No way. No way. On a good day, she hated to shop. In two-inch heels, it was stilettocide. "You think I can be beneficial?"

Again he looked her over. "Don't know, but Anthony said something about Marshall Fields. I hate Marshall Fields. On the other hand, your sparkling companionship could get me through it."

Mickey turned away, turned away from the dark, compelling eyes. Turned away from that mobile mouth that seemed to be terminally amused. She was halfway to the door when she heard his low voice. Deep, sexy words that tickled their way down her spine, one vertebra at a time.

"See you tonight—sweet cheeks."

THE AISLES OF MARSHALL FIELDS were not where a virile, all-American man should be on a Saturday evening. It was embarrassing, emasculating and damned shameful. Still, Anthony's son needed a wedding present, and Dom was determined to find something appropriate, yet suitably tough, no pantywaist gewgaws from him.

"Maybe we should get a bottle of Scotch?" he suggested.

"Are they registered here?" Michelle asked, surprising him with what she knew.

It was one surprise after another with her. She had showed up in front of the station in a dress that knocked him in the gut. It wasn't her usual tacky outfit, not that it was demure, either. This dress smacked of sexuality. Some white silk thing that was cut short, so short it made a man itch to explore exactly how short it was. Michelle wasn't stacked, but nicely curvy up top. Again, she just looked—right. If he ever got her naked, he'd spend about two hours just memorizing all her lines.

He stopped so suddenly that Michelle crashed into him.

"Are they registered?" she repeated, as if he was a moron.

It primed his ego and made him want to act like the stupidity was a farce. As if "getting naked" thoughts couldn't get him dead. "How do I know if they're registered?" he asked, mentally undressing that long body once more.

He kept forgetting why he had wanted her here in the first place. To figure out exactly who she was.

She shrugged one elegant shoulder. "They just tell you."

Dom tried to remember exactly what Anthony had said about the wedding. "Don't know."

"We can check," she answered, and moved toward the china department as if she knew just where she was going. Who the hell was she? She walked awkwardly in her heels, looking as if she was unused to the usual busyness of every female he had ever met. Yet, damn, could she kiss. Still he could remember how she felt, how her lips parted so effortlessly. He shot a quick sideways look at her. Maybe somebody had brought out their big guns. One of those innocent-looking broads with the high-powered starters that knew men, and knew sex. Maybe "they"—whoever "they" were— knew Dom's weak spot. Okay, it was every man's weak spot, but still...

He followed her blindly into a demilitarized zone known as the bridal registry. As she walked, he found himself slowing, watching the swing in her hips, watching the long length of her legs. She was tall. Almost as tall as he was. Her bare shoulders emerged from the white silk. Pale, not tanned like a lot of the girls he knew. The blond mane had to be fake, but there was no disguising that face. It was lean, angular and the dark-framed glasses were a great touch. They gave her an air of arrogance—and mystery. Dom had always loved mysteries. It always got him in trouble. That, and poor judgment.

Michelle stopped in front of the kiosk decorated in roses and bells. "Here we are. What's the bride's name?"

Dom thought for a minute. "Mona."

She tapped her foot. "Do you know Mona's last name?"

What did she think? He was doing time with Anthony's future daughter-in-law? "No."

"Perhaps you know the groom."

"Sure. Testa."

"Is that a last name or a first name?" she drawled.

Playing with her was starting to get fun. "Last."

He watched her fingers fly across the keyboard, like a secretary or something. She sure as hell knew how to type. He was a hunt-and-pecker when typing was required.

"Here it is." With a single flourish of her finger, papers started flying out the hole in the bottom, and she handed him the list. "Crystal by Waterford, Dolmen, and china by Royal Albert. Hartington. Good stuff."

"Okay," he said, like he knew what she was talking about.

"Do you see a salesgirl?"

Dom looked around the empty store. "No." He put two fingers in his mouth and whistled. The sound echoed in the quiet corridors, and one or two shoppers poked their heads out to stare.

Michelle glared at him, and for the first time he realized her eyes were blue. A sky blue that was barely noticeable behind her thick lenses. Right now they were noticeable because she was staring daggers at him. Obviously whistling was not the right way to flag a clerk.

"Don't you ever shop?"

Dom shrugged. "Not if I can help it."

She turned on her heel and gave him her back. Whoever she belonged to, he must be loaded. She knew the right brand names and she walked around without looking at the directory. This was a place she was used to, so he supposed he should trust her taste. "What do you think I should get?"

"How much did you want to spend?" she asked, neatly rattling him even more.

Oh, that was a tough one. His budget was tight, and he'd rather spend his money on graft and corruption than dinnerware, but he needed to make an impression. And he needed to look like he had money—but not too much money. "A couple of hundred." That seemed safe.

"Go for the Hartington."

An older saleswoman appeared, clad entirely in red. "May I help you?"

Michelle didn't even hesitate. "We'll take the gravy boat."

"Would you like that wrapped or delivered?"

"Wrapped," interjected Dom. He didn't dare show up without a gift, even if it meant being late. Bad move.

Michelle shook her head, the blond curls moving as one. "It's going to take a while."

If he was lucky, they'd miss the entire wedding ceremony. "We can wait."

"It'll take half an hour, young man. Our gift-wrapping service is quite comprehensive."

Dom checked the time. Thirty minutes was perfect. "'S all right. We'll wait." He turned to Michelle. "We'll get a cup of coffee."

After paying for the gift and making arrangements for the "proper" bows and crap, they headed down to the Walnut Café. The dining room was more a place for women who had too much time on their hands. Dom sipped his coffee and watched Mickey, wondering if this was her element. "So what do you do in your spare time?" he asked, his curiosity rearing its head once more.

"Read. TV. Movies."

Almost normal. Except for that reading thing. Dom couldn't remember the last time he had picked up a book. Course, most wise guys wouldn't be caught dead with a tome in their hands. "I like movies."

She smiled at him politely, as if to say, "That's nice, but not in your wildest dreams."

Damn she knew how to step right on a guy's more honorable intentions. Or maybe they weren't so honorable, but he figured if she was a plant, then she knew what was what. He would be expected to make a play for her. It was all about the game.

He just couldn't forget that it was nothing more than a game. She was fascinating, intriguing and just a little clunky, and the combination whetted his appetite like no woman he'd met in a long while.

The idea of spending long hours in her company, merely unwrapping her package—both in the figurative and literal sense—awakened something inside him, something that he'd kept dormant for a long time. Of course, that's probably exactly what they'd figured he'd do, pegging him for the horny bastard that he was. Undercover work was hard on a man's sex life. People really had no idea.

"Do you think you can try for the tape tomorrow?"

Ah, yes, the mysterious tape. It was always about the

tape. To be honest, he wasn't sure it existed. "I'll go look on Monday when the scammer's at work."

"Maybe you could try tonight?"

"I thought your friend would be home tonight," he said, wondering if he was supposed to get caught breaking and entering. It was a stupid setup, but guys had been brought down by lesser slipups.

She crossed her legs in front of her, the skirt riding up exquisitely high. Once again her packaging was calling to him, parts of him responding right on cue. Damn.

"Probably," she said, all casual like. "Monday then. Here's a cell-phone number. One of those disposable jobbers that can't be traced, so don't even think that it's legit."

He cracked a smile. "Whoa. Looks like you've covered all the bases."

"Of course I did."

"Why's the tape so important?"

"It should never have been made."

That was new. "It was one of those foot or farm animal things? You're trying to be an actress, aren't you?" He hoped that wasn't true, because she'd never make it.

"An actress? What do you think I am? Some vacuous bimbo who can't do anything more? You men are all alike."

Dom hid his smile. The brain thing seemed to be a sticking point with her. "I've got a bad case of primordial regression."

"Good. As long as you understand."

"Sure." He stood, thought about helping her up, but she looked so militant, so determined to be on her own, he just watched instead. "Ready to head out?"

She uncurled her legs from the small table, and he felt a twinge of something that was probably sympathy. Whatever got her here, she wasn't happy about it. For just a second, her walk was brisk, no-nonsense, and then she glanced back.

He smiled at her open look of assessment.

The walk shifted, the hips swayed and he found himself watching once more. It wasn't pretty, but damned if he wasn't getting more than a little randy just by watching that eye-glazing swing. There was an odd rhythm. Just when you thought you had the beat, she gave it an extra ka-ching.

There couldn't be much harm in a guy noticing a woman's moves, could there? The voice that had kept Dom alive for the past two years had some objections, but content to watch the sway and pitch, Dom chose not to listen.

MICKEY SWORE QUIETLY to herself. The sandals were giving her a blister. She'd dressed nice tonight. Sexy, but nice. And every time she looked at Dominic, he was watching her with that speculative look, but she wasn't so stupid that she didn't notice the heat in the look, as well. And that was really ticking her off.

The clingy clothes and the long blond hair called into every male stereotypical fantasy. That fantasy was sooooo not Mickey, nor would it ever be. The other reason she was annoyed was that—well, that she *was* annoyed. It shouldn't bother her. Nor should it thrill her. But it did and she wasn't sure which was worse nor, to be honest, did she really care. She just needed the tape, and then this whole charade would be over.

And she'd never see Dominic Corlucci again.

Which brought in a whole new wave of emotions, which annoyed her even further. She looked back over her shoulder, noticed the Saturday-night smile. "Can you hurry it up?"

"Sorry," was all he said, and they made it up the steps to the back of the chapel.

They had ended up at the church with about ten minutes to spare. Dominic drove a Honda, which seemed a little odd. She was expecting something bigger, something less fuel efficient. Not a Honda four-door that looked like it couldn't hold golf clubs in the trunk, much less a body. But what did she know? If you cut off the head and legs, the human torso really wasn't that long.

As they were rushed to some seats in the back, the sounds of the wedding march began, and everybody stood. It was a traditional Catholic wedding, striking up memories of Jessica's recent nuptials. At least Jessica would be back in another week, although Mickey had pretty much decided to keep most everything to herself. It was one thing unloading her mistakes to Beth, who seemed to think the whole thing was a spectacular adventure, but it was another to admit weakness to Jessica, who would never, ever let her forget it.

The bride looked gorgeous, happy and content. Really content. Mickey wanted to holler out to her, "You're marrying a wise guy. Is this what you're reducing yourself to?" but wisely she held her tongue.

Stubbornly she looked around the chapel, looking anywhere but at Dominic. He looked good in his suit. Better than she wanted him to look. Mickey always prided herself on focusing on more than just the outer facade of the human appearance. A man's mind was more important than a great set of abs. It was an edict that was easy to believe in when you were exposed to receding hairlines and physiques that were less than ideal. Confronted with such godlike physical attributes, it seemed shallow and a full-frontal betrayal of all her principles to be filled with lust.

Careful not to get caught, she gave him a quick once-over. Yeah, definitely lust. Black was his color. When contrasted with the dark line of his jacket, his hair shone without color at all. The truest black that swallowed up all the light around it.

*And his mouth.* This man had a mouth that should have been feminine. Should have made him look prissy. Instead, that mouth made her stop breathing. Wide, full, expressive lips. He was always moving them. Smiling, frowning, smirking. Like he knew about his effect on women. The cad.

He almost caught her ogling him, but she covered and concentrated on the stained-glass window just on the other side of him.

The church was packed with dark-haired men, perfectly coiffed women and screaming kids. Every now and then, one goombah type or another would nod in Dom's direction. He'd send an answering nod, some sort of mob fraternity handshake.

Why couldn't she be afraid of him? It was a mystery that she wasn't going to solve right now, but as soon as she got home, she was going to sentence herself to six hours with Joe Pesci and *GoodFellas.*

Nothing like a little blood and gore to put the fear of God into a female.

Finally the ceremony was over, and she could concentrate on more important things, like walking in her heels.

The reception was a few blocks away and—of course—they walked. He made a point of putting her on the inside of the sidewalk. A nice touch, but she really needed more help with the walking.

The dress and the shoes were Cassandra's. And while the dress was okay, the shoes were one size too small. She stumbled, and he grabbed her arm. It was only one touch. A polite, impersonal touch. But her body just responded with its own law of attraction. The force operating between two masses is equal to the two masses multiplied together, preferably in a carnal manner. Then the result was divided by the square of the too few inches between them. Lastly, the whole disaster was now multiplied by the Corlucci sexiness constant. Sadly, the constant was in triple digits.

For a moment she leaned in, using gravity as an excuse to get close. He looked into her eyes, and Mickey felt her flesh go even weaker.

"You doing okay?" he asked, as they entered the small hall, and suddenly they weren't alone anymore. Mickey straightened, focused on the pain in her foot and condemned all males to perdition.

Yeah, that was easy, she thought to herself, ignoring the little snickering from the peanut gallery in her brain.

The reception hall was lit with candles and roses. Except for the one-hundred or so mafiosi, it would have been really romantic. Two weddings in less than two weeks. Her life was cursed. She shot a sideways look at Dom, looking sinfully delicious, and decided being cursed wasn't without its rewards. He led her over to the bar and ordered two glasses of cabernet.

For a few minutes they stood, listening to the music, and she sipped her wine. He left his untouched.

Then the band kicked into a soulful version of "Speak Softly, Love," and Dom put down his glass.

"Want to dance?"

She didn't want to, her feet were killing her, and as much as she had flashed JUST PRETEND in front of his eyes, the look he was sending her was flashing another sort of signal. Sadly she shook her head. "I can't."

He shrugged. "Suit yourself, although it'll look weird if we're the only ones sitting out all the dances."

Then he stared ahead, his dark eyes sad and sorrowful, as if she'd stomped up and down on his favorite toy. Men.

"Oh, all right," she said, trying to convince herself that she just wanted to do him a favor. Yes, officer, that's Mickey Coleman aiding and abetting the mob. Why? He was cute.

But when she slid into his arms, the world drifted away. He didn't have to ask her to move closer, her body did that for her. He didn't have to ask her to press his cheek so close to hers. There wasn't a part of her that wasn't completely enveloped by the hard confines of his body, by the clean scent that he exuded, by the sure warmth of his touch. Around the crowded dance floor they moved, so effortlessly that Mickey forgot her sore feet, she forgot her common sense. For one dance, she would lose herself with him.

"It's not so awful, is it?" he asked, his mouth mere millimeters away from her ear.

And Mickey Coleman, woman of a thousand stars with a master's in astrophysics en route to a doctorate, an IQ of 175 and knowledge of more cosmic events than Superman ever dreamed of, began to purr.

# 4

THERE ARE SOME WOMEN that a man is destined to distrust. Women who wear disguises for instance. Women who pretend to be one thing, but in reality are another.

Yet with Michelle in his arms, Dom found his distrust slipping away right in time with the music, one soft beat after another.

She was trouble, he knew it. But his brain just couldn't wrap itself around the logical facts. Possibly because his brain didn't seem to be working at all.

Right now, he wanted to be away from this place, alone with her, just the two of them. Something normal, rather than at a wedding reception that contained the vast majority of the Chicago Outfit—including Vincent Amarante, aka the Boss.

Everyone here had nicknames and secret lives that no one knew about. Including Dom, including Michelle. And he hated that. For once he wanted to be normal, wanted to be alone with a woman, no disguises, discovering all the idiotic little bits of trivia that color the lines of someone else's life. These were the things that a man and woman did together when they were normal. And he couldn't because he was carrying a phony ID and an unregistered weapon, and she was wearing fake hair.

The song changed to something faster, peppier, but he ignored it, letting everyone else dance around them.

Screw 'em all.

Dominic pulled her closer, listening to the soft humming sound that was coming from low in her throat, memorizing her perfume and wondering what it was. It was spicy, almost masculine in its scent. On her skin, it was like bottled sex. When he fell asleep tonight, he was going to remember that scent—if he fell asleep.

In the corner, a collection of men huddled around the bar, Vinny the Boss in the middle. Dom knew this was his chance. His opportunity to just slip right in and become one of the guys. Trusted.

He knew how it worked. He'd been in the center once before, and it was a mistake he was still paying for.

The smell of cigars was stifling, and the complete, unsuspicious warmth of Michelle was seducing him away from all sense of duty. For once, couldn't he just pretend to be the good guy?

The voices were buzzing around the room like flies in August, and he wished he could tell them to just get the hell away from both of them. When he was a kid and he'd gotten angry, he'd punch the wall, or his brothers, or whatever else seemed to be in his path. Unfortunately you just couldn't punch the whole world.

Instead, he saw the exit sign beckoning across the floor, signaling an escape. Dom maneuvered them around the floor, closer and closer to that blessed door.

The song ended just as they found themselves outside. It was an alley, backed up to an abandoned ball field, not the most romantic place in the world, but Dom had never wanted to be anywhere more.

Here was away, a safe haven, where for half an hour, two hours, a whole damned lifetime, Dominic Cordano walked a straight line. His alter identity, Dominic Corlucci, he was the man whose walk was a little bent.

They strolled over to the ballpark, and she leaned against a long-forgotten bleacher where SO loved JH 4ever.

"I hope you don't mind," he said, shrugging off his jacket and handing it to her. "Smoke bothers me."

She looked up at him, wide eyes staring behind her glasses, trusting and thoughtful. For a woman with fake hair, she wasn't any good at hiding her emotions, and for that he considered himself lucky. Then she smiled up at him, nervous and unsure of herself, and he felt himself transported to another world where they were alone.

There was one last thing he needed to make sure of. One more question he needed to ask. "Why did you come to me? Who told you?"

She blinked, once, twice, thinking of what she was going to say. Finally, she must have figured it out. "A friend of mine works there. She's scared of you. She figured if she was, then Monihan would be, as well. She's a good friend."

So the explanation was as simple as that. She wasn't a plant, just a woman who needed rescuing.

"Thanks for escaping out here with me," he said.

"I like being outside. Just looking at the sky," she answered, her wistful voice soothing away the last remnants of his anger. She stared up, beyond the street lamps into the night sky where the crescent moon hung overhead.

"It's big," he said, and winced at the stupid remark.

"Over a hundred-billion stars," she answered and he blinked.

"Wow, I never would have guessed that."

She lifted an arm and pointed up, to a spot far away from every wise guy in Chicago. "There's Venus and the moon, just lined up. See?"

He moved in close behind her, his gaze tracking the length of her arm, until he could see the single bright light that was sitting just on the left hand of the moon.

When she lowered her arm, he stayed where he was, fascinated by her, by her absolute absorption in the stars. "You like your astronomy," he said.

She took a step back, so near to him that he could simply breathe and his chest would brush against her back. "It keeps things in perspective."

Oh, yeah, he knew where this was going. "The 'you're just a grain of sand on the beach of humanity' theory?"

She shook her head, and he wanted to know what color hair lay underneath her wig. "No," she answered. "There are constants and there are subtle shifts that are always evolving. The universe expands, time slows or increases, but it doesn't matter what the changes are. The rotation about the sun, the orbit of the moon, those don't change. It's a great fusion of dynamic and static forces all working together in concert."

He had no idea what she was talking about, but he could listen to her voice for hours. It wasn't drugs or penny-ante larceny, or even who was winning at the races. Her words were a little bent, but this was the closest thing to a normal conversation he'd had in two years and he realized how much he missed it. "A philosopher, as well as an astronomer," he murmured.

"That's not philosophy, that's physics."

"Who are you?" he asked and she turned.

"Someone you wouldn't want to know," she answered, brushing a piece of fake hair out of her eyes.

"What if I do?"

At his considering stare, she turned and looked back up at the sky, as if all the answers could be found there. "This isn't my world, you know," she said, like she was from another place or another time.

It wasn't her world, but she thought it was his. Dom swore under his breath. He ached to tell her that this wasn't his world, either. Unfortunately, if he were to be honest with himself, this was his world. It had always been his world, and no matter how hard he ran, he couldn't escape it. He shook off his past and pulled out his knife and carefully carved her name in the grayed wood. Very precisely he worked, one letter at a time. An age-old practice of letting the world know that you cared.

She watched him work with fascination. "That's me, isn't it?" she breathed quietly.

Dominic lifted his shoulders. Maybe he shouldn't have done it. Maybe it seemed high school to her. But he wanted to have some of his innocence back, and she was giving him that, whether she realized it or not.

When he was done, he hesitated, wanting to put his name under her own, linking them together. Unfortunately, those sorts of gestures—permanent and way too visible—could be dangerous for her. That was a risk he wasn't willing to take, but there was another way.

"Michelle?" he asked, a wealth of meaning in simply saying her name. He wasn't asking for much, merely one taste, one sip from a cup that he shouldn't have.

She sighed and he found himself holding his breath, waiting desperately for her answer.

"Please," he said, his heart pumping inside him. She didn't realize how important this was, how much he needed to rediscover that piece of ordinary life inside him. He'd been living a lie for so long, it was taking over him, slowly and surely.

*Only one kiss.* That's all he needed from her. One kiss, one meeting of lips, just to feel clean. Just to remember.

Whether it was the pleading in his voice, or the stars, or the damnable forces that were working between them, he didn't know, and he didn't care. All that mattered was that she turned to him and lifted her head, and he didn't wait to think about it anymore.

He knew what she tasted like, had remembered that one kiss from the coffee shop, but that was pretend. This was real.

Her face felt so small in his hands, and his mouth took hers quickly before she changed her mind. Whatever magic this night possessed, he could taste it on her, drink from it, and he did. Her arms curled around his neck, and her body curved into his, fitting them together more strongly than he had ever imagined.

Far away a lone siren blared above the low strains of the music, but Dom ignored it. While the irredeemable world carried on, he found himself fascinated by the warm caverns of her mouth, reveling in the absolute redemption of a single kiss.

She was beyond seductive, no pretense or coy games,

just her. His body wanted her so badly, a touch, a possession and release, but Dom was too afraid to move, too afraid that with one small misstep, the illusion would return, and he'd lose himself once more.

Time slowed, just as she had said, and he did nothing but kiss her. She didn't ask or complicate things, she understood, and for that he loved her. For once he didn't have to pretend, or be someone else, he could simply be.

With each passing second, he felt himself returning. He remembered feelings that he had forgotten, and found himself reveling in something that was actually good. Something that was honest and true. The freedom, the escape was just as seductive as her.

*Wham.*

The door slammed open against the brick wall, and angry voices emerged, a dunking of cold water on a warm summer night. A reminder of who he was and who he wasn't.

Dom pulled back and his fleeting glimpse of another life slipped through his fingers. He pasted the emotionless look of calculation back on his face. His soul-sucking world had swallowed him whole.

Michelle stared up at him, her lips swollen and parted, and from the corner of her forehead, a lock of dark hair had emerged. A forcible reminder that no one was who they seemed. That gritty truth put a particularly bitter taste in his mouth.

Two shadows danced in the doorway. Another woman and another man.

''You asshole! If you ever, ever, come dragging your

lousy, two-timing, conniving, 'oh, baby, come on' butt back home again—''

*Crraack.*

It was a fist coming in close contact with flesh, probably a nose. Dominic's hands bunched in automatic response, and he felt the familiar surge of adrenaline rush through his body, heating his blood. One, two, three...he concentrated on the count, forcing his anger to cool.

Dom knew that sound well, and listened as the woman's fury turned into tears.

That was the crappy thing about the bad guys—they didn't rush to rescue anybody. Only fools rushed in.

Mickey stirred, ready to rush in, but Dom held her back. This was his job. His world. Just another day at the office, honey. When you were looking to nail Vinny Amarante for racketeering, you just couldn't go up and punch him in the face, no matter how much you wanted to.

Vinny's wife, Amber, emerged from the shadowy doorway first. Against her face was a red-soaked tissue, and her shoulders were shaking from her sobs. The door slammed shut behind her, leaving Amber alone in the night. Apparently Vinny believed that his wife had received his message loud and clear. Michelle walked over to her, pulling a tissue package from her purse and silently handing it to the woman.

Not knowing what else to do, Dom positioned himself at the door. He wasn't any good at comforting females, didn't understand tears or mush, but he did know how to watch somebody's back. For tonight, that somebody was Michelle.

MICKEY HAD NEVER in her life seen so much blood. Well, once, when Davey Ward had gotten bit by a neighborhood stray in second grade, but that was it.

She put an arm around the hysterical woman and tried her best to calm her.

"What's your name?" she asked, hoping conversation might stop the tears.

"Amber."

"Oh, that's a pretty name. Was that your boyfriend who did this to you, Amber?"

Amber sniffed. "My husband. The son of a bitch. You know, you think he'd have the decency to carry on his affairs in private. Someplace where I'm not, but noooo...."

Husband wasn't good. That meant they lived together. Although nowadays, divorce was easy— Mickey shook her head. "You can't go back home with him. Let's take you to a hospital."

"I don't need no stinkin' hospitals. It's not broken. Just bleeding like a mother." Amber sopped at her face with the tissue.

"Well, you can't go home," Mickey pointed out patiently.

"I'm doing what I always do. Get a room at the Hilton and let Vinny go out of his freaking mind with worry."

It all sounded so routine, so normal, so...wrong. "You're not going back to him, are you?" she asked, trying to keep the judgment out of her voice.

Amber didn't even think before she answered. "I don't have another home. I loved him at one time. That's got to be enough."

Mickey tried to think of words, but failed. Boyfriend problems she could handle; employment woes, she could help you out. But this? This was a whole new galaxy. "Do you want to talk about it?"

"No, I can't," Amber said, starting back inside.

"Don't go back. Stay and talk. We're not going anywhere, are we?" She flashed Dominic a bright smile and he nodded. "See?"

"It's an ugly story," Amber said, but she was inching farther away from the door. Some progress.

"If it involves a man, it's always ugly."

"Oh, that is so true." And there, pressed against the ragged brick wall, Amber started to talk.

Sometimes she burst into tears. Sometimes she rambled, and lots of times she cried. Mickey patted her arm and nodded in all the right spots, but she really didn't know what else to do. So she listened. Eventually Amber's tears dried up, and her voice calmed.

Then she picked up her purse and looked ready to go back inside, as if nothing had ever happened.

Quickly Mickey intervened. "Uh, don't you think you need to get away for tonight?"

Amber looked at her and smiled. "You're a sweet girl to be so concerned for a stranger. Especially listening to me whine about my life. Unfortunately, this is all I have." She wiped her eyes with her hands and turned to Dominic. "You treat her nice, you understand?"

Dominic nodded and took charge. He made a quick phone call and then took out some bills from his wallet and handed them to Amber. "Go get cleaned up, take a hot shower and maybe some whiskey for dessert. Cab should be here in a minute."

"Amber, they have places you can go," Mickey said, lapsing into stereotypical schmaltz, but she didn't do sensitivity well.

"Uh, no, Missy. But thank you for caring. That seems so rare these days and all."

Mickey wished that Dom would back her up on this, but the man she had kissed earlier was long gone. Standing in front of her was a cleanup man, a man used to mopping up everybody else's messes.

Silently they walked over to the corner just as the cab arrived. Dom bundled Amber into the cab, packing up all the crises in the world and then shutting the door. Why couldn't he care more?

Mickey watched the taillights from the yellow cab pull away and turned to Dom. "Why didn't you try to convince her? She should leave him, go into a shelter."

His mouth twisted into a hard line and he jammed his hands into his pockets. "This is Chicago, Dorothy, not Kansas. God knows I can't stop people from making stupid choices. I can only make them more comfortable while they're doing it."

It seemed such a defeatist attitude. He'd just given up. She felt like whacking him one herself. "I can't believe you're going to let her go back to that bastard."

One lonely streetlight shone down on him, and even dressed up in suit and jacket, he fit in with the surroundings. It was his casual acceptance that hurt her most of all.

Stupid, Mickey, very stupid. She wheeled around and walked away from him. Right now she needed to be far away. Why had she thought she could pull this off? Because he kissed her? Because every now and then he looked at her with those deep, soulful eyes?

No.

When he looked at her, she felt desired and feminine and needed. When she looked in his eyes, she saw a vision of herself reflected back. A woman she'd never known before.

As they had walked down the street, he had deliberately switched places, so that he was walking on the outside. On the dance floor, he had been so protective, ensuring that no one bumped into her.

In her whole entire life, no one had ever considered that Mickey Coleman might want someone to take care of her. Just once.

For just a few hours—a few measly hours, how pathetic was that?—she'd been the most fragile woman in the world.

Unfortunately, reality was starting to intrude.

He caught her with a hand to the arm. "Michelle, don't."

"You're a coward," she snapped, angry with Vinny for being an ass, angry with Amber for being so stupid and angry with Dominic most of all, because he should have been better than this.

He should have been noble and courageous and more rescuecentric. Instead, he was acting like—a wise guy.

Hell-o! Wake-up call to Michelle Cushing Coleman.

And no one ever said that Mickey Coleman was stupid. Ever. She spotted a cab and flagged it down, and then, thank God, the taxi pulled next to the curb. She didn't dare look at Dominic, because she'd lose her nerve, let him flash those deep pools of brown in her direction.

She concentrated on opening the darn door, but the stupid thing wouldn't cooperate. Finally, she ripped it open, nearly dislocating her shoulder in the process.

"Good night, Dominic. No, make that goodbye."

FOR ALL INTENTS and purposes, Dom should have let her go. Let her disappear back to where she came from. He didn't need the additional pressure. Frankly he didn't need the guilt, either. He hated the guilt, because it was slowly eating him alive.

It would be the smart thing to just stand here, or maybe put his fist in a wall, but the old tried-and-true Cordano methods weren't enough. She'd stirred something inside him, something more than his jones. He couldn't let her walk away. Not now.

When he was with her, when he kissed her, he felt like an honest man. He could remember that he was a cop—a good cop. It all felt right. It was the way he was supposed to feel.

No way in hell he was letting her get away.

He opened the door and climbed in beside her.

The cabbie shrugged. "Where to, Mac?"

Michelle glared at Dominic over those thick-framed glasses, and he couldn't help but smile. "Leave me alone," she said through gritted teeth.

Damn, he loved it when she tried to take charge. "We're not done."

"We're done," she said, giving him a regal staredown. He was starting to recognize that look. She could teach a few professional killers the art of being cold.

The driver, obviously sympathizing with the usual male sufferings, turned up the radio.

"I think we need to clarify a few things—" he started.

"I'm not having this conversation in a cab."

He abandoned attempts at a rational argument. "So let me take you home."

"No!"

Rational arguments weren't working, either. "Okay, maybe not home, but at least let me drive you back to the train station."

"I'm not stupid," she said, her fingers tapping on the purse in her lap.

Dom was content to wait her out. "Nobody said you were."

"You should have helped her. You should have done *something*."

And how could he explain his life to her? It was the life he wanted when he was a kid. It was the life his brother wanted, too.

He grabbed at the medal around his neck, praying for wisdom. Not surprisingly, wisdom stayed absent. So Dominic did what he did best. He lied. "Michelle, I'm a practical man of business. If I'm going to get my ass kicked and she's still going to go back with him in the morning, tell me what I've accomplished other than getting my ass kicked?"

"You can look yourself in the mirror."

That was below the belt. He didn't look in the mirror anymore. He didn't have to feign the ice in his voice. "Oh, yeah, and then I'd consider myself a moron. They have these fights every time the moon is full, and she still loves him, and she still goes back to him, no matter what the hell I say."

"How can you live with yourself? She's going to get killed."

Dom closed his eyes, trying to shut out the words. He couldn't really live with himself. Survived was the better word. He touched the medal at his neck and closed his eyes, needing the strength. Nobody was ever going to die again.

Unfortunately, the Outfit had a way of being hazardous to one's health. Which was one of the primary reasons that she shouldn't be here, near him. She shouldn't be here at all.

So why was she here? Because, God forgive him, he couldn't resist.

"What are you going to do, Dominic?" she asked, and honestly, he didn't know. But he could answer her question about Amber—that one was easy.

"I swear, Michelle, I'll do everything I can to protect her."

She studied him, and he held firm. This was a promise he could keep. And it felt good to do something noble for once. Maybe a man really could change.

If he were truly honorable, he'd climb out of the cab and tell her to get away from him. Go back to wherever the hell she came from. She was just some woman that needed his help. That was a laugh. What could he do?

*Go away, Michelle,* he thought to himself. But the words never made it to his tongue, and his body didn't move.

Eventually her fingers stopped drumming on the

bag, and she sighed. "Take me to the corner of Kline and Oakmont. My car's parked at the bakery."

Dom grabbed her hand and pulled her out of the cab before she changed her mind, then he passed a twenty to the cabbie for his time and support.

Relief was the only emotion smacking his brain. The guilt had disappeared. Out of the corner of his eye, he watched her. The hair was slightly askew, the arms were crossed tight across her stomach. Unapproachable.

While he drove her back to her car, he contemplated the various conversations he could start. Politics, sports, the latest Hollywood blockbuster.

Whether she considered criminal involvement a fatal character flaw and a detriment to a relationship.

*Or sex.*

He steadied himself and tried to concentrate on the driving.

There was road repaving just south of I-57, and he sneaked a couple of more glances her way. Now she was curled down into the passenger seat, looking more little girl lost than anything else. He wished he were a photographer and he had some way to capture the line of her jaw, the angle of her cheek forever.

It was her contrast that got to him. She was all hard and punchy, with a skirt that was more not-there than there. But inside her, there was this vulnerability, some sort of insecurity, and that was what boggled his mind.

So what did she have to be insecure about? If he had her smarts, he would be on top of the world. But when he saw her eyebrows draw together, when the glasses slid down, he wanted to draw her close, cup the curve of her cheek and taste her again.

Wanted to make everything all right for her.

The car inched forward—the red trail of taillights beaming ahead, and Dominic was secretly thrilled that a simple lane closure could give him a few more minutes with Michelle.

"Thank you for coming tonight," he said. It wasn't a goodbye, wasn't even close.

"You're welcome," she answered softly.

He pulled off into the shopping center, and she directed him to the Mazda convertible with SKY SPY on her plates. Oh, Michelle, you're making this too easy, he thought to himself.

In five minutes or less he could find out who she was, find out where she lived, find out what she had for dinner last night. If he could do it, so could anyone else, and with the crowd she was currently hanging with— namely him—it was the "anyone else" that scared him.

He worked over the words in his brain. An easy excuse to duck out of the deal. Sorry, but it's been fun. Don't call me, I'll call you. There were a million ways to make her forget him, but he was going to ignore them all.

He walked her to her car, telling his conscience to shut up, and therefore proving his theory that perhaps Dominic Cordano wasn't the good guy he wanted to believe that he was.

She stopped next to the door and searched the sky.

"You see that?" she asked, pointing to a blinking spot of light. Every time she looked up there, she had such intensity in her face.

Dom looked over her head and found the satellite. "That a plane or a satellite?"

"It's a falling star."

Now Dom hadn't been born yesterday, but tonight was all about pretend. And if she really bought the falling-star stories, then he would play along. "So is that good luck or bad luck?"

"Your wish is supposed to come true," she said, in a voice that said she still believed such superstitious crap.

"I don't think my wish is gonna come true tonight," he murmured, focusing on her mouth. And then he got momentarily lost in a fantasy that involved losing the fake hair and tangling the sheets, with long kisses that lasted the night.

She met his eyes and he found his desire reflected there. "I don't think mine is, either."

"You're asking for trouble," he said, giving her a last warning. "You should walk away from me."

"When I have the tape," she answered easily. Too easily. Did she realize that he couldn't just leave her alone?

He changed the subject to something safer. "Monihan's gone on Monday a.m.?"

"Yeah."

"I'll check it out."

"I would appreciate that."

The cool night air blew her hair back, exposing the dark locks just at her forehead. Why couldn't she trust him with the truth? He wanted to see what she really looked like, wanted to touch her again to see if it was like that every time.

He was spinning dangerously out of control whenever she was within touching distance. Maybe it was nothing more than the night.

Yeah, right.

"Don't slap me," was all he said, and then he met her lips and took her. Hot and forceful, letting her know how much he wanted her. This was the Dom that everyone knew. The self-centered bastard who was always on the make. He wanted her clinging to him, needing him as much as he needed her. She didn't disappoint. Her mouth opened, her tongue mingling, matching him stroke for stroke.

Didn't she know who he was?

When he lifted his head, she was smiling. "You think you stole that kiss? Maybe I should ask for my money back, because you're not much of a thief."

This time he put his all into it. His tongue swept deep inside her mouth, angry, taunting her, needing her to stay away. He found the small dot of frosting left on her upper lip. Tasted the last drops of wine that she had at the reception. Tasted the inherent innocence of her. It was a taste that raced through his blood, dulling his anger.

Wanting more, he delved deeper, pulling her tight against him, her breasts crushed against his chest. Her legs parted, and he took advantage, pushing his thigh between hers, her skirt rising to death-defying levels.

Someday those legs were going to wrap about him, he thought, and heard himself moan.

His hands cupped her butt, keeping her locked firmly in place. His erection pressed hard against her softness, but still he needed her closer. Needed to be inside her, buried deep, deep inside her, where she couldn't run away.

She wasn't helping the problem. He was dying here, and the way she was rubbing against him was more than he could take.

He pressed her against the car door, his hands sliding beneath her skirt—

A car honked, teenagers yelling at them, and he broke free. Another couple of minutes, and he really wouldn't have cared who was watching. Good job, Dom.

"What are you doing to me?" she asked, a blush covering her cheeks as she straightened her skirt.

God only knew what was going on between them. Dominic had wanted women before, but never like this. He had always been in control. Always able to walk away. Once a year he allowed himself one night to ease his frustrations and that was the end of it.

Now he plastered an easygoing smile on his face. "Payback, dollface. Someday soon, good night will not be an option."

She got into her car and started the engine, and he stood alone, watching to make sure that she got away safely. Just as she pulled out, she rolled down the window and looked at him. Even behind the thick glasses, he saw the need.

His hands fisted; *Ave Maria piena di grazia*, he recited to himself, struggling for control. He could not do this. Not to her. Everything he touched, he ruined.

He told himself that he could handle her. Just find the tape and get her safely out of your life, Corlucci. You've got a job.

Slowly he got into his car, but he didn't turn on the motor. Instead he sat and looked up at the sky.

The cold, hard fact was that he couldn't wait to see her again, and that was a problem.

# 5

On Sunday morning, Dom awoke after having a most amazingly realistic dream about one Michelle Jones.

First thing on his list was to discover Miss Jones's true identity, and for that he needed to make a call. A call from a pay phone a few untraceable blocks away.

In only fifteen minutes, through the computer hoo-doo magic of the Chicago Police Department, he had his surprising answer. Considering what his gut had told him about her, maybe it wasn't surprising at all.

SKY SPY, alias Michelle "Foxy" Jones, was none other than Michelle Cushing Coleman, who rented a two-bedroom apartment in Schaumburg. Her current employer was Astrophysical Sciences Research Center, she had three bank accounts at Chase and one speeding ticket from May 2001.

Her education credentials actually scared him. There was an undergraduate degree in physics and a master's degree in astrophysics from U of C. Her father lived on the north side, where Michelle had been born. She had a mother, who had been reported missing in the fall of '77, and turned up in San Francisco living with a music composer in the fall of '79, after which Andrew Coleman, a prominent heart surgeon, had promptly filed for divorce. Not exactly a criminal history. Other than the speeding ticket and a mysterious tape, Michelle Coleman was a perfect law-abiding citizen.

As he walked down the busy sidewalk, the El roared overhead and he smiled to himself. Michelle Coleman was not a Mafia mole, nor a prostitute, nor a corrupt person of any kind.

She was normal. Everyday, average, normal. Well, okay, she did get blackmailed with sex tapes. But he didn't care because, quite simply, when he was with her, she reminded him of who he wanted to be. Then Dom turned around, walked back to the pay phone just outside the local convenience store and dialed.

"Dad?"

"Domenico! *Figlio,* it's good to hear your voice. Where are you this month?"

"Oregon. Got a load of televisions to haul and then I'm heading back to Florida."

"What? They don't have enough televisions in the world? You should come home to see the family. It's been too long."

"I know, I know. How's Mom?"

"She is good. She tells me I should be walking. Me! Walking! I tell her to go away and leave me in peace. But still she goes on, and goes on, and goes on."

Dominic smiled. "And Christopher? He's not in trouble?"

"Not today, but tomorrow? Ask me tomorrow. He stays out all night—like a hoodlum—and I tell him find some silly girl to move in with like his friends. Then we won't worry. He tells me I'm a crotchety old man and still he stays out. The bum. I worry that about him,

Nico. I've lost one of my sons to this city. I will not lose another."

Dominic leaned against the wall, the ache in his belly squeezing like a mother.

"Dominic? Are you there?"

"I'm here, Dad. Just tired, that's all." He wondered if he could tell his father the truth. Would his father forgive him? Probably not.

"Get some sleep. They talk about the truck drivers on Channel Seven. They say truckers never sleep. You sleep?"

"Yes, Dad," answered Dominic, relieved to hear the sadness disappear from his father's voice. "I miss you, Dad," he said, and he wondered if it was time to tell them the truth about his life. At eighteen, he'd left New York to go someplace new, walk new streets, see new faces. Escape. He'd never thought about being a cop before, but he figured that he had dodged the law too long. It was time to make amends.

He didn't tell his family because they didn't approve of cops. After Tony's accident, the word *police* was never mentioned in the Cordano household. Besides, Dom was used to hiding things from his family. He told them he was a truck driver and the lie had stuck. Same as all the other lies.

"You come home. We'll see if you can still beat your old man. I don't think so. You grow soft. Your mother asks about her grandbabies. She's not getting any younger."

Dom laughed. "Not yet. But I met a girl."

"Ah! So that is what you're calling for. You're married and we weren't even invited."

Dom cracked a smile. "No, I don't think so. You'll all get an invitation."

"Good. That is what a good son should do. Can you tell me her name?"

He stayed silent, thinking if he said it aloud, it would be ruined. But he wanted to share something with his family, something good, something that didn't involve lies or laws. "It's Michelle."

"Michelle. It's nice. You should bring her east for Christmas."

"It's too early to tell, Dad." Dominic would have to rescue her tape first.

"You're my son. You're a Cordano. That's all you need."

It was going to take more than the Cordano charm to win her over. Working for the mob was a big strike against him. As much as he wanted to pretend otherwise, for now, this was his life. Somebody had to clean up the bad guys in the world. "Maybe, Dad. Maybe."

"You'll talk to your mother? She's out getting her hair done, but I could have her call you back."

"No. Give her my love." In another half hour, Dom would be incommunicado, notably staking out one John Monihan. It wasn't tracking down terrorists, but a man had to atone for his sins one step at a time.

"You should do that in person."

"I'll be home soon, Dad. As soon as I can." Maybe he shouldn't have called, but he was starting to feel like there was another life that he had. It felt fresh and clean. The dirt he'd dragged around for so long was starting to disappear.

Dom hung up the phone and then took the stairs to

the red-line platform. Now he was going over to the South Side, to stake out the scene of the crime. Because tomorrow he had a tape to steal.

FIRST THING ON Sunday morning, Mickey called her dad. Just to remind him about the presentation. Just to tell him about her latest article in the *Journal*.

Dad wasn't home.

She left a message and hung up, but then spent a good bit of time staring at the phone. Very odd. Sometimes he was caught in emergency surgery, but on Sundays he was usually lying in bed reading *The Sun-Times*.

Not that it was a huge mystery. And she had more important things to ponder.

Like Dominic.

The man was trouble.

She heaved herself out of bed, watered her plants, paying special attention to Lucretia, who was looking very, very droopy. African violets were so touchy.

Then she called Beth because being alone was dangerous in her current state of mind. She needed a voice of reason to keep her from doing something stupid. Mickey wasn't exactly sure if Beth was the voice of reason, but when times were desperate, standards could be lowered.

An hour later she was at Beth's apartment, playing computer geek. She showed Beth the ins and outs of IM and e-mail, the neat tricks you could do with word processing and how to make a pie chart with spreadsheets.

"Oh, look! It's a genuine Spode." Seemed that Beth was a natural for eBay. Oh, the joy.

"Which Spode?" asked Mickey, flipping channels until she found the Cubs game on WGN.

"The blue Italian mini-oval teapot, and it includes a pasta bowl. You wouldn't believe how rare these things are! And it's only eighteen dollars and forty cents for both."

Mickey murmured something appropriate and settled in to watch some baseball. Out of all the things to get excited about, a teapot?

Beth let out a gasp. "Would you look at that? Come here!"

"What is it?" murmured Mickey, having just gotten comfortable on the big, overstuffed couch, while Corey Patterson was up to bat.

"Male strippers. Live."

Strippers? Mickey tried to feign disinterest, but she did turn around to sneak a peek. "You're too repressed, Beth."

"I know, but I found this link from someone's weight loss site." Bad porno music filled the room, enough to turn off anyone's libido. Mickey's interest returned to the game, where she just missed a double play. Once again, undone by wanton appetites. There was a message here—she just needed to pay attention to it.

"How did it go with the mysterious Mr. Corlucci?"

"Good," Mickey answered, feeling another wanton urge pulse through her, just at the mere thought of him. She frowned.

"Good? Is that all you're going to say?" Beth asked, sounding just like Jessica. And that was all it took.

The dam burst.

"You should have warned me," Mickey said, shutting out her old favorite pastime, baseball, and concentrating on her new favorite pastime, Dominic.

Beth's smile turned all female. It was an odd moment, seeing a vamp look on little innocent Beth. "Studalicious, definitely."

"I'm going nuts. You'd think I'd learn from the last miserable experience," Mickey said, honestly more of a whine, but she felt entitled.

Beth put her fingertips to her forehead. "Stop right there. I'm sensing scoopage. I know that I'm not the J-woman, but just consider me a poor substitute until Friday when she gets back. I need to live vicariously." She fanned herself two-handed style, and then sighed. "Okay, go on. I'm ready."

Mickey braced herself for the big moment of confession. She got up, paced three circles around the couch and wondered if she should really bare her soul. It seemed so awful. Finally, she just blurted it out. "I went to a wedding with him."

Beth's face fell. "I thought at the very least that sex was involved."

"It was a nice wedding," answered Mickey, now feeling like a failure. "And I did think about sex. A lot." Then she smiled a smile most feline. "And he did, too."

"You want him," Beth said, and Mickey flopped back down onto the couch.

"You're supposed to be the voice of reason, not leading me to the dark side."

"He's in the Family," answered Beth, playing the part of the cautious friend.

"Oh, shut up," said Mickey, playing the part of a bitch.

"Now wait just a minute here. That's my best voice of reason. It doesn't get more reasonable than that. You're an astrophysicist, for God's sake. Get smart."

"I hate myself," said Mickey, as she pulled a needle-point pillow over her head. "I want to see him again. Just to talk—maybe. Why can't I learn from the big old wonking past mistake that I'm *still* paying for?"

Beth got up and retrieved a bowl of carrots from the kitchen, and then flopped down in the chair across from Mickey. "I don't think you can put Dominic and John in the same category. He doesn't seem like the kind of man who would blackmail you for sex."

"No, because he's too busy killing people."

"We really don't know that," said Beth, crunching thoughtfully.

"You're deviating off the path of reasonableness."

"Okay. We'll stick to the facts. What happened last night? What crimes were committed?"

She retold the events of last evening, leading up to Amber, omitting some of the heat of the kiss. "There's this poor woman, physically abused by this jerkola, and did I stay up all night with worry, wondering if she would end up maimed? No. You know what I thought about all night?"

Beth smiled, a devilish smile. "Yes."

"What should I do?" said Mickey, the prehistoric woman's cry which roughly translates to "I know what I want to do, and it's not what I should do."

"Go for it," said Beth without hesitation.

"He's one of the Family," Mickey shot back, clinging desperately to Beth's own argument.

"Someday you can write a book about the whole ex-

perience and make a fortune. *I Was a Mobster's Moll.*
They could have a TV movie about the whole thing.
With Susan Lucci!''

"You write about it, Beth.''

"Maybe I will.''

"Don't you dare.''

Beth waved a hand. "Oh, don't worry. Maybe I could
write it up for one of those true-story magazines.''

Mickey looked into Beth's innocent blue eyes. And
for the first time she noticed it. Sneakiness, deviousness,
intrigue. How cool was that?

There were untold depths that she'd never suspected.
"Oh, my God. You've done it, haven't you?''

Beth blushed nicely, although the sneakiness didn't
completely disappear. "A few. The money's good. I
need something to pay the rent.''

"No way! What did you write?'' asked Mickey, sitting up to hear more.

"'I Was a Mail-Order Bride.' 'Turned on to my Pool
Boy' 'Play Toy—Diary of a Bored Housewife.' 'My
Mother-In-Law Tried to Murder Me,''' answered Beth,
picking up a stick of celery and munching.

"How come you didn't tell anybody?''

Beth shrugged. "It's not something you brag about.''

An awful thought occurred. "Have you written anything true?''

"Oh, please! Does everyone always think that fiction
is based on real people? Uh, no. True life is not that interesting.'' Beth glanced at Mickey. "Well, most of the
time.''

"You swear you won't write about this?''

Beth crossed herself, Playtex style. "I swear.''

"I keep thinking I'm stupid for actually liking him. He seems nice."

"He always says 'thank you' and 'please' when he orders his coffee."

"If I did pursue a relationship with him—a purely superficial affair because obviously I can't get involved with him romantically—would you tell anybody?"

"Not if you didn't want me to. He might not be a criminal. Maybe he's just hanging with the wrong crowd. A victim of poor social judgment. I've never actually seen him do anything illegal. You could have a private detective investigate him, find out if he's got a record or anything."

"No, Beth, hiring out is what got me in this mess in the first place."

"No. That was Monihan."

"Please don't mention the name of the unmentionable evil one. Dominic's just got to get that tape tomorrow. I keep putting him off, and putting him off, and he keeps pulling me back in."

"Dominic?"

"Monihan."

"He'll get it."

"I hope so."

"You got to have faith, Mickey."

Sadly, Mickey shook her head. Beth was so naive. "No, Beth. Lesson number one for a full and independent life, don't have faith in anyone else. You can only depend on yourself to get things done."

Beth laughed. "I have to depend on other people, or I'd never get *anything* done."

"It's that sort of defeatist attitude that will bog you down," said Mickey, shaking her head sadly.

"I don't know. I'm not smart."

That kind of patented self-pity just made Mickey mad. "But you've got looks. With looks, smarts aren't that important."

"Says the woman with the greener grass," said Beth snippily. And that from a woman who *never* got snippy.

Mickey rolled her eyes. "You really think women with brains can get further than women with looks and/or charm?"

"Every time," said Beth.

Arguing with Beth was about as productive as splitting quarks. "You know how to do IM, right?"

"Of course," answered Beth.

"Good. And you have to mark yourself 'away' if you're really away." It was the height of embarrassment to send out messages to empty air. What if you were being ignored on purpose?

"I can remember that," said Beth.

"Too bad you don't have a computer at Starbucks."

"Don't get any ideas."

Mickey sighed. "I know. I'll be happy when Jessica gets back."

Beth looked insulted, and Mickey realized that she stuck her foot in it. "But *you* are going to get all the juicy details on Dom, not her."

"You're going to do it, aren't you?" asked Beth, the devil in her eyes.

Slowly Mickey nodded. A load had just been lifted from her shoulders. It wasn't smart, but it'd be a once-in-a-lifetime opportunity. Something to tell the grand-kids, or most likely, the grandkittens. To have grand-kids, she'd have to have children, and to have children, at least in Mickey's Code of Conduct, she had to have a husband, and to have a husband, she had to meet—and be attracted to—a man of high moral precepts.

None of which was likely, considering her current track record. All the more reason to just give over to the hedonistic pleasure of doing Dom.

Then she leaned back into the pillows and smiled. "Not do *it*, Beth. Do *him*."

# 6

MONDAY WAS NEVER Dominic's favorite day of the week. It was currently 6:00 a.m., and he was eyeing the cup of coffee with bleary-eyed suspicion. When he was growing up, Sunday had always been the day of rest at the Cordano household. Due to the long hours of Saturday evenings, it was usually needed. Leftover resting on Monday was pretty common, as well.

Much to his mother's disappointment, school had never been his thing, and his high school in Bensonhurst wasn't really conducive to education. At least not book smarts. He learned all sorts of useful tricks. Breaking and entering, hot-wiring cars and how to make fake IDs.

He shut his eyes and downed the rest of the coffee. The past was dead.

Today there were three things on his to-do list. A meeting with Frankie at Dilly's this morning. Second, breaking into Monihan's apartment right about lunchtime and finally, stealing a tape, if the thing existed. Now see, this was the problem with hanging with the bad guys. You didn't believe in anything, anymore.

But lately things were starting to change. He felt different. Happier. Cleaner. *More like a human being.*

All because of her.

One Michelle Coleman, with eyes that made you feel like a man. Okay, he had to say that her long, lean body made him feel like a man, too. One very randy man.

He threw himself into the shower, allowing five extra minutes of extended sexual fantasies. Which was absolutely the last he was going to think about her, because trouble had a way of following in Dominic's footsteps. And one Michelle Coleman didn't need the sludge of his life oozing into her own.

And to make sure that he kept his word, he did an extra two litanies, which in his mother's words, were better insurance than Allstate.

DILLY'S WAS A COMBINATION deli-pool hall near Comiskey Park. A lot of cops thought it was old school and out of business, but Dom was learning otherwise.

The Chicago Crime Commission made sure there was always someone keeping the Outfit in check. It wasn't the most glamorous assignment. Capone was only a bedtime story. Nowadays the criminals stayed low and kept out of the papers.

Dominic liked it. Nobody believed the investigation into possible construction kickbacks would amount to anything, except for Dominic and his captain.

He walked inside, and a few construction workers were waiting at the counter for breakfast. Old man Dilly was slicing lox and pouring coffee, and Frankie was sitting at a table in the back, reading the morning paper.

Thinking better of mainlining any more caffeine, Dominic bought a pint of orange juice and then pulled up a chair. "Morning, Frankie."

Frankie scowled over the top of the paper, his reading glasses making him look more like somebody's father than a second-class mobster. "Do I look cheerful and happy to you? Devilish Wings tanked in the fifth. God, I could make glue out of that horse myself."

Dominic pulled his face into a suitably serious look. "I told you that Jiminez was running him too hard. You should have gone with Tough Luck. Twelve to one."

"With my luck, he'd have lost anyway."

Dominic took a swig of the OJ, all casual like. "You just need something to turn it around, Frankie."

Frankie shook out the paper and continued reading. "I ain't superstitious."

Time to bait the hook. "I might have just the thing."

Frankie paused in his reading. "What?"

Dominic pretended to stall and carefully scoped out the room. "I got a whole batch of ATM cards, passwords included, for sale. I thought this might be a good time to include a partner. Maybe bring Vinny in on the deal if he wants."

"You've always been quiet about your deals before. Why not now?" asked Frankie, his eyes distrusting.

This was the tricky part. Dom couldn't look too open, but he didn't want to be too cagey, either. "You want to know the truth?" he asked.

"Yeah."

"I think I could help you."

"You don't need to be feeling sorry for me. I do fine on my own."

"Well, I know you're having a bad run, and things have been flush for me recently. My own endeavors have prospered nicely."

Frankie nodded. "That's very thoughtful, but I'm betting that right around September, I'll be having a change of fortune."

"Something good?" asked Dominic, trying not to seem too overeager.

"Very lucrative, if you catch my meaning."

Frankie was holding his cards close and it was too soon to pry, so Dominic stole the sports section and pretended to read. "You're entitled to good things. I'm glad to hear it."

"Can I ask you some advice?"

Intrigued, Dominic lowered the paper. "Sure."

"You're a winner with the ladies."

Dom shrugged his shoulders, disappointed in the change of subject.

"There's a certain lady who has caught my eye, but I'm not sure how I should approach her."

"She been giving you the look?"

"What look?" asked Frankie blankly.

Dom felt a surge of real pity for the big guy. "You know, intense, lots of eyebrow action, little smiles."

"No. She don't really know I exist."

Dominic blew out a breath. "That's a problem, Frank."

"Don't I know it," said Frankie, pushing up his glasses.

"You talked to her, asked her out?"

"I talk to her, we chitchat about the horses."

"Does she seem interested in the horses?" asked Dominic, figuring this was Frankie's mistake.

"No."

"What is she interested in?"

"How should I know?"

"You have to ask."

"Oh," said Frankie with a considering nod.

Dominic put aside the paper and leaned forward. "Can I make a suggestion?"

"I would be happy if you did."

"Send her flowers."

Frankie frowned, his eyebrows knitting into one. "I'm not sure if I should do that."

"Why not?"

For a minute, Frankie thought in silence. "It's not really my style, you know? I wouldn't know a rose from a gardenia."

"Give her flowers," insisted Dom.

"What if she doesn't like me? I'd never be able to show my face around her again."

"Just sign the card 'From your secret admirer'. She'll love it, and you can ask her about it later. Say you heard she received some flowers anonymously, and you can get her reaction and she'll never know it was you."

A lightbulb went off in Frankie's eyes. "Whoa. I could do that, couldn't I? Lends the whole thing an air of mystery and intrigue. The ladies go for that?"

"They love that," said Dominic, pretending that he knew. He didn't have a clue and wasn't any closer to understanding the female psyche. After all, he was the poor sap that was massively intrigued by a woman who didn't trust him with her real name.

Frankie put down the paper and beamed. "You're a good friend. Want to play some pool?"

Dominic polished off his juice and then picked out a cue stick. "We betting on this game?"

Frankie grinned, showing more teeth than a shark. It was going to be an expensive morning. "Of course."

Dominic watched as the big guy prepared to break. Frankie was ready to trust him with his love life, but not his business. When Dominic had taken the case, nobody thought much of it. Everybody said the Outfit was dead. Dominic thought otherwise and he wanted to prove it.

Now he was on his way to doing just that. Frankie was a captain, and one level up the food chain. If Dominic could help Frankie snag his mystery woman, then that could be his way deeper inside.

Frankie cleared the table before Dominic even had a chance, but Dominic paid up with a smile. The day was looking bright after all.

AFTER LEAVING DILLY'S, he donned his Chicago ConEd hat and shirt, in case of prying eyes. But there was no one around when he found Monihan's apartment.

And Monihan lived in a dump, he thought to himself as he surveyed the three-story walk-up. As he made his way upstairs, the steps creaked, but all was quiet. It was a good day for a break-in.

Illegal entry was a talent that Dom had acquired in high school, and he had yet to meet a building he couldn't penetrate. If locks didn't work, there were windows. The criminal element was Dom's best talent. Unfortunately not all Cordanos were duly blessed. His brother had sucked at it.

Dominic felt for the cold medal around his neck, and pressed the silver deep into his flesh. Pain was always preferable to guilt.

Now was time to go to work.

A single door lock protected the door, no dead bolt, probably not a security chain, either. This town was a dangerous place without the proper protection. He made a mental note to himself to call Michelle and talk to her about proper apartment security. Surely an astrophysicist would have a dead bolt at the very least.

And, on that note, he made it inside. Just as Michelle had said, Monihan wasn't home. Other than her name and true identity, which was a biggie, she'd been telling him the truth. He had wanted to believe her, wanted to think that he could trust her now. Wanted to think that maybe—at least on her side—they could dispense with the lies. As soon as he got the tape back, that is.

So he went to work and searched the place. Next to the TV were several unmarked videotapes, so Dom sat down to fast-forward through them, trying to maintain a professional attitude. He'd avoided thinking about this part, actually watching the tape. It'd be like betraying Michelle's trust, but he didn't have a choice. It's not like Monihan was going to label it: "Sex with Michelle."

And the sex fantasies were back, only Monihan was nowhere in the picture. Just Dominic and Michelle. A very naked Michelle.

Dominic whapped himself on the forehead. Mind out of gutter, please.

Then he went through six videos, which contained several episodes of *24* and the last few innings of the Giants game. No Michelle at all.

He was frustrated and really wanted to hit something, but that wasn't going to solve anything, so he continued his search in the kitchen. Patience wasn't his strong point, which was why he became an under cover cop.

The coffee table was piled high with books, and Monihan's choice of literature was certainly enlightening. *Spies of the Soviet Union, The History of Extortion, 37 Sure-Fire Plots* and some more how-to books on writing mysteries.

So Monihan was writing spy novels. Interesting, but not illegal.

Dominic turned on the computer and started poking through the files. There were a handful of video files there. Movie clips, music videos and one striptease clip, but unless Michelle had bazoomed into Pamela Sue Anderson, it wasn't the one he was looking for. Further down, he found two-hundred files labeled Chapter One. He stopped reading after Chapter1-Number10.doc. These were bad. So bad that he laughed in several places. He'd remember that for when he talked to Michelle. It'd be nice to make her laugh, because his search wasn't going to make her happy. If Monihan had a tape, it wasn't here.

*If there was a tape.*

Maybe Monihan had lied to Michelle. She said that she had *heard* the tape, but she didn't say she'd seen it.

After one last look around the apartment, Dominic left, allowing himself one painfully hard punch at the door.

The call to Michelle was quick and businesslike. He heard the disappointment in her voice, and he wished he were a better cop.

"Dominic?"

"Yes, sweet cheeks?" he answered, hoping she'd laugh.

She didn't. "You'll keep looking, won't you?"

"Your lack of trust is killing me here," he said, even while he wondered if she was lying to him.

"Please keep trying."

"I will," he promised. "I'm on the case, Michelle. Don't do anything stupid."

"I won't," she said.

But Dominic knew that tone. Instead of tailing John Monihan, it was time to follow Michelle. He wanted to protect her and keep her out of trouble, because she had that tone in her voice and he'd heard it once before. It'd been a long, long time ago but he still remembered. Last time, his gut had told him something was wrong and he blew it off. This time, he wasn't going to let anything bad happen. Not again.

MICKEY HUNG UP the phone and peered over her computer at the jerkola. She'd been so sure that Dominic could get the tape back. Yeah, Mickey, good job. Depend on someone else to do what you need to do yourself. How many times had her father told her that no one could do anything better than her? For a few days it'd been enticing to think that she could lean on someone else. Use their strength instead of her own.

Now it was time to turn into superwoman again.

She took a deep, steadying breath and then got up to approach the enemy.

"Whatwillittaketogetthetapeback?" she asked, not breathing until she had every vile syllable out of her mouth.

John looked up in surprise. Then he smiled, one of those "I'm a nice guy" smiles that was really at odds with his current character. "Once more should cover it."

"Just once?" asked Mickey, making sure the terms were clear here.

"Yeah, it's research."

*Research? Oh, yeah, that's rich.* "That is such a smarmy answer," she snapped. "Where's the tape?"

John looked at his computer and smiled. "The wonders of a digital age."

"You copied it, didn't you?" asked Mickey, for a clear moment contemplating murder. Would a jury convict? Probably.

John looked up at her, innocent like. "Maybe."

For now, she needed a bit more information. Just a few more clues, Watson, and the case would be solved. "If I put you in the happy place, you'll delete the file? No, better yet, I'll delete the file." Mickey leaned over and grabbed his mouse. "Show me which one it is."

John smiled and even pointed. "Right there. You can delete that one."

She hit the delete key with a flourish, but unfortunately he was still smiling. *It is never that easy, Watson.* "It's on your home computer, too, isn't it?"

"Yes."

However, computers were only as secure as the people who manned them. Mickey kept her smile to herself, adopting her girlie-girl persona. "Okay. I'll be over at your apartment tonight. Nine o'clock."

"You remember where I live?"

"Yes."

"Don't be late," he said arrogantly, and then went back to work, effectively dismissing her.

Mickey wanted to deck him, but she restrained herself. Physical violence wouldn't solve anything. No, the solution to the situation involved much more cerebral thinking.

She checked her watch. Five hours left.

Thirty minutes later, she hit upon the solution. Once again, her brains had come to the rescue. She spent the remainder of the afternoon at her computer, running the compiler until everything was perfect.

It was a good feeling to be back in control again.

Never underestimate the power of one very ticked-off woman.

DOMINIC PARKED OUTSIDE the entrance to the labs and watched as Monihan's beat-up Mustang exited the parking lot. Michelle's Miata was still parked in the lot. Looked like she was working late tonight.

Well, he had no choice but to wait. He pushed the seat back as far as it would go and made himself comfortable. He skimmed the dial, finally turning to NPR. The dulcet tones of the broadcaster began the interview with a highbrow geek who was convinced the universe was expanding and apparently he had the data to prove it.

It was interesting, although Dominic was skeptical, but he wanted to see what Michelle saw when she looked up in the sky. He needed to find something beyond the world that he had made for himself.

Finally, at seven-thirty, it happened. He got his first legit look at Michelle Cushing Coleman. She'd lost the blond wig. In reality, her hair was dark and straight and swung around her shoulders when she walked. Exactly right for the thin, angular face. Tonight she was missing the bimbo outfit, instead wearing a practical cotton button-down with thigh-hugging jeans that clung in all the right places. She wasn't a woman he normally would have noticed, but now he couldn't tear his eyes away from her.

This is who she was when she wasn't with him.

So why pretend to be someone else?

Dominic laughed to himself. He knew the answers to that question. *Because you have something to hide. Because nobody else was ever going to guess your secrets.* But Michelle was different from him. Her secrets weren't nearly as bad as his own.

As she pulled away from the parking lot he cranked his engine, and eased in two car-lengths behind her.

They headed east on 64, and kept going east past her turn onto 59. She pulled onto 290 and went south, right into the south side of Chicago.

He slammed his hand against the steering wheel. Why couldn't she have trusted him to handle things? For a smart woman, she was about to do something really stupid. She was going right toward the home of one John Monihan. He called and postponed his meeting with Anthony. Tonight he had something more important to do.

Michelle needed him, whether she realized it or not.

# 7

THINGS WERE GOING exactly as she had planned. John was currently in the kitchen calling for Chinese food. She'd given him that frank, appraising look that she'd seen Cassandra give men, and told him that she wanted to eat first, and maybe a glass of wine, as well. After he handed her an unopened bottle of chardonnay, he'd scurried off like a worker ant. Men were so simplistic.

After that, she settled herself in front of his computer and found several video files on his hard drive. Aha! Just as she started to check them out, John called out from the kitchen.

"They'll be here in twenty minutes. I opened some wine."

Mickey jammed the disk into the floppy drive and stood to watch as the virus did its thing.

Just as the skull and crossbones came up on the screen—she'd designed it herself—John came into the room.

The evil laugh played over the tinny speaker.

"What did you just do?" he said in a strangled voice.

Mickey put her hands on her hips, warrior-princess style, and smirked. If only she had a camera, then she could savor this moment forever. "I'm doing what I should have done a long time ago."

"What did you do?" repeated John, running to the computer and pounding on the keyboard. "My files are gone."

"Bloody right, they are."

"All that hard work. What have you done?" He looked completely horrified, as if she'd just blown up the universe.

And did he really think she felt sorry? Uh, hello. "I'm not about to be manhandled by some vile insectoid."

"You bitch!" John got up and advanced, and Mickey picked up the bottle of wine, ready to use it as a weapon if necessary.

Suddenly, there was an explosion of glass and the window burst, followed by a dark figure.

It was Dominic, brushing glass off his sleeve. "I don't think so," he said, coming to stand between Mickey and Monihan.

"Who're you?" asked John.

Mickey began to smile. Dominic was tall and right now he looked really mean. She'd never truly appreciated the art of physical intimidation before now. A purely primitive tingle cruised down her spine.

"Somebody who's really pissed off at you, Monihan. Where's the tape?" Dominic turned to Mickey. "Like the hair, dollface."

Mickey clapped a hand to her head. The wig! Oh my gosh, he hadn't seen her real hair before.

John seemed to have more important things on his mind. "I can't believe this. You've destroyed four years of my life. There is no stinkin' tape! I was writing a book. A thriller. Guy blackmails girl, she murders him, then has to cover it up. I wanted to see how far you would go. It was research. For. My. Book."

Mickey gaped and glared and searched for the exact perfect words to curse this man for the rest of his adult life—to give him boils and warts and all sorts of frog-like manifestations. Finding no words, she punched him in the stomach instead.

Monihan doubled over, groaning a little but seeming more concerned with protecting his gut.

Dominic nodded with approval. "Remind me never to tick you off."

"Do you know how long I've been working on those manuscripts? All that work," moaned John.

For Mickey it was icing on the cake. She, who never yelled, began to yell. "Do I look like I care? You were blackmailing me with a nonexistent tape!"

"You are such a bitch."

Dom backed him up against the wall and, in a match of muscle, Mickey was betting on Dominic. "You don't want *me* to hit you," he said in this low, growly voice that made her insides go metaphysical—in a good way.

"He's connected," said Mickey, as she crossed her arms across her chest. This was better than anything Al Pacino had ever done.

Dom laid his arm across John's throat and turned to look at her. "It's your call. I could break his legs."

"No, no!" cried John. The wuss.

"You're going to blackmail women again, John?" said Dominic.

"No. I swear. You want me to, and I'll leave town."

"Really?" These words were music to Mickey's ears. "What do you think?" she asked Dominic.

"I think I should break his legs," he answered with the absolute cutest smile.

Mickey pretended to consider it, all the while watching John sweat. Finally she sighed. "You are my hero, but no."

Dom shrugged. "Okay. You're free. This town's not big enough for the two of us." He turned to Mickey and grinned. "I've always wanted to say that."

"I'll leave tomorrow," said John. It was about time he saw the writing on the wall, but she wasn't done yet.

"Tonight," she snapped. "I'll turn you in to Dr. Kartesian on ethics violations alone."

"You don't have any proof I was doing anything."

Heh-heh-heh. With a flourish, Mickey pulled out her pocket tape recorder and pressed Play. John's threats echoed in the room. "Remember, John. Always have a backup plan."

He hung his head low. "I'll be gone as soon as I pack up," he said.

Dominic dusted his hands. "And once again, justice triumphs. Ready to leave, dollface?"

"Yeah, let's get out of here." Mickey picked up the bottle of wine, and then took one last look at John. Finally, it was over.

As they walked to the door, Dominic's warm hand found Mickey's. "Say that again," he said, so low she almost missed it.

"Yeah, let's get out of here," she repeated, more than a little confused.

Just as they reached the bottom of the stairs, he stopped her. "No, the part about being your hero."

The entryway was dark, with only a dim streetlight

coming in from outside. Still, the light was enough to see him clearly, to see the vulnerability in his eyes. Every now and then, she saw what lay beneath the surface, and it was that small piece of him that he kept so hidden that called so strongly to her. Probably another stupid mistake, but she wasn't going to walk away. "You *are* my hero."

"I kinda like that," he said with a nervous laugh. Then the embarrassment cleared and he tugged gently at her hair. "Don't ever wear a wig."

He looked as if he really *liked* the way she looked. It wasn't as if she was ugly or anything, but she certainly couldn't compete with Cassandra or Jessica or Beth. "It's okay? I mean, well, this is who I am," she said, hating the whiny tone in her voice. She despised women who weren't secure in their own self-image, and she had no reason to complain. Her gifts just weren't the usual combination of blond hair and blue eyes, capped with a J. Lo butt. Unfortunately, she had no butt at all.

He didn't seem to mind. He shook his head and looked at her, really looked at her. "I want to hear all about Michelle Cushing Coleman. Everything. From the moment you were born until the time you discovered you could write computer viruses and do all sorts of cool stuff with atoms and the cosmos."

He knew. She stared, openmouthed at him. It probably wasn't her most elegant look, but she couldn't help it. "How did you find out?"

"I've got my sources," was all he said as he opened the doorway and followed her out. It was a beautiful night, clear and full of quasars that sheared through the black sky.

It was a night when names were forgotten, potential felonies were not to be mentioned, and nothing was allowed but the overwhelming need that was surging inside her. He looked at her like she was the only female in the world. Never—absolutely never—had a man looked at her that way. Her heart took over, because her brain had stopped.

It was ten o'clock, and she was more than ready to cross over the line. "Come home with me?" she whispered.

He stopped and pulled her around to face him. "You mean that?"

"Come home with me," she said, her voice more sure.

"Now, tomorrow, anytime," he answered.

Her heart pounded as their gazes locked. Suddenly she realized exactly what she'd done. Pandora's box had come open, and Pandora wasn't about to shut it, either.

"So you like brainy women?" she asked, wanting to make a joke but failing.

"I think it's sexy as hell, and if you start whispering about neutrinos, I think I might just bust my pants right here," he answered in the same light tone, but the look in his eyes was downright nuclear.

"My vocabulary is pretty unlimited," she said, moving closer, feeling daring and exquisitely female.

Then she was in his arms, his mouth driving into hers, and she didn't care. He had the most perfect mouth, tempting and playful one minute, intent and demanding the next.

There was something dizzying about his desire. It

was so raw, so genuine. Her legs went queasy, ceasing to hold her up, and he backed her against the lamppost. There she was, all his muscle—mob-tied muscle—pressing into her.

She should be pulling away, issuing a discreet "hands off" cough, doing something. What did she do? She curled her arms around his neck just so she could bury her fingertips in the hairs that grew at his nape.

Idiot!

His hands wandered beneath her shirt, pressing against the soft skin at her back, exploring the curves of her butt, pressing her even closer.

Moron!

Mickey moaned. Tonight she just wanted to feel. To be swept away in an undertow of passion. Now she knew what it was like. Low, insidious, pulling at her like the most powerful magnetic field.

When he dragged his mouth away from hers, she groaned. "Don't do that to me," he whispered.

"What?"

"Public indecency. It's a Class A misdemeanor in this city. You go home. I'll follow."

"We could ride together," she said, unwilling to part from him. It was a long ride back to Schaumburg.

He kissed her quickly. "Another dangerous idea. When I get you alone, I want you in a place where naked and willing is not a crime."

Mickey sighed, but obediently spent the next forty-five minutes driving in her car, alone, contemplating the many aspects of naked and willing.

MICHELLE'S APARTMENT was bright and green—forest green. There were climbing vines, minitrees, plants and flowers. Not one brown leaf in sight. Everything looked vibrant and alive.

Dom took in the rest of the details, memorizing it all. On the walls were diplomas and awards and pictures of her friends. His walls had always been bare. She had a stereo and a rack full of CDs. He'd just never taken the time. He settled on the sofa and pretended he was comfortable.

"Want a beer?" she asked as she headed off into the kitchen.

"Just water," he yelled. As a rule, he didn't drink; alcohol had a bad way of making him talk.

A few seconds later, she returned and handed him a glass.

"You sure got a lot of plants," he said, needing to make casual conversation.

"They take the carbon dioxide out of the air. It's actually very healthy to have them around."

He shook his head. "I just kill them."

"You need the right plant. An ivy or a dieffenbachia. Indestructible."

She was so naive. "I could kill it."

"Next time…" she started to say before trailing off.

His hand clenched the glass and he looked away, studying the certificates on the wall. There wasn't going to be a next time, and they both knew it. Why was he doing this?

"You know, I could go—" he said, standing up to leave.

"Don't."

Her one quiet word had him sitting back down.

On the drive over, he'd had a chance to figure out exactly what he needed to say. He shouldn't be here, he knew that. Shouldn't be contemplating making love to her, he knew that, too. But in the last three years, he'd had so few times to feel human, to remember who he was. It was selfish and dangerous, but he couldn't resist. He told himself it would just be one night. After all, now that Monihan was leaving, and there was no tape, there was no reason for her to need him anymore.

Which left him feeling hollow, empty and ticked off as hell.

When she sat down next to him, looked up at him with trust, the uncomfortableness factor zoomed ever upward. People really shouldn't trust him.

So he got up and began to pace. It seemed easier than looking in her face, watching all that good and trust flowing all over the place. "Are you sure about this? About me?" he said, man enough to ask but not man enough to leave.

She took her time to answer, as if she was picking her words carefully. He steeled himself for rejection. It probably would be best, especially for her.

"You have a good heart. A kind heart. I don't know about your career choices—we'll have that discussion later—but no one has ever done what you just did for me."

Once again he began to breathe. Okay, life was looking up. He'd probably go to hell for this, but it'd be worth it.

"What did I do for you?" he asked. As far as he knew, she had handled everything pretty much on her own. He'd done squat.

Michelle fiddled with her glasses, drank two long sips of water and, in general, kept him waiting far too long for his answer. Finally she spoke. "No one's ever watched out for me or protected me. I was always the smart one. Able to do everything. And tonight I discovered the luxury of letting somebody else do it."

"Well, you did do a good bit. The virus was a masterstroke," he said, needing to point out the obvious.

She came and stood next to him, her hand stroking his arm. Everywhere she touched, he started to burn.

"We make a good team, don't we?" she asked, unbuttoning his shirt.

Part of him was dying to touch her, but part of him knew that he was pulling her into a place that she didn't belong. He stood silent, not stopping her, but not touching her, either. It was a compromise that he could live with.

Her fingers slid along his shoulders, the shirt falling to the floor. The air cooled his overheated skin, her light touches driving him slowly and purposefully insane.

"Where'd you get that scar?" she asked, tracing the line across his arm, her eyes alight with curiosity.

It was an innocent question, and he had a well-rehearsed answer waiting on his tongue. Everyone else had been told that it came when he did two years in Joliet. Just another prison brawl.

She didn't press him, but waited patiently, her eyes still holding that godforsaken trust.

"I ran into a tree on a motorcycle when I was sixteen," he said, the truth spilling out without any influence of alcohol at all. He needed to earn the trust that was shading her eyes.

"You could have been killed," she murmured.

"I was wearing a helmet."

She traced the line of red flesh with her lips.

"You have any scars?" he asked, struggling to breathe.

"I had my appendix out when I was thirteen. There's a little scar there," she said, her eyes dancing behind her glasses.

It felt so good, so normal to be standing next to her, and Dominic gave up the fight. Slowly he unbuttoned her shirt, exposing her bare skin inch by inch. He eased the shirt off her shoulders, letting it fall to the floor, and she stood before him dressed in jeans and a sensible white cotton bra.

Rediscovering a talent long buried, he unhooked the fastener at the back with a single snap. She was gorgeous. Her skin was the color of peaches, her nipples dark and erect.

She was absolutely perfect, so Dominic gave her one last chance before the perfection was gone.

"This is it, Michelle. If you're going to come to your senses, do it now, because I don't think I can stop." It was a silly thing to say. He knew he had to have her. Guys like him weren't known for their unselfish attitudes. But it made him feel less tainted to say the words.

She didn't answer, just smiled. A wanton, sly smile that told him everything he needed to know. For tonight at least, she was his.

Now he wanted to see all of her.

The jeans were taken care of, then the white cotton panties. Very practical packaging for such a long, marvelous body. Her curves were subtle and fluid, and trapped his gaze more completely than any pinup.

The traces of mischief disappeared from her eyes, replaced by nervousness. One of her feet crept demurely over the other, like covering her toes made her less vulnerable.

He hated to see her weakness, because it pricked at his conscience. He needed her strong.

"You are so exquisite," he said with complete honesty. His hands cupped her shoulder, then slid down her arms, trapping her so that she wouldn't leave him.

Looking pleased, she smiled. "So are you."

Slowly he shook his head. "I meant all of you."

Behind the glass lenses, her light blue eyes were tender, so wonderfully tender. She leaned forward and softly met his lips. "I did, too."

Dominic chose not to argue. She had papers published in magazines he couldn't even read. Someday she was going to have long lines of initials after her name. It seemed easier to just believe her.

Doing his best to play the part, he picked her up and carried her into the other room, laying her down on the small bed.

She cleared a spot on her nightstand, right next to *The Long History of Neutrinos*—a little light reading. Then she took off her glasses and laid them down.

It was the first time he'd seen her eyes without the layer of glass between them. They were softer, and gentler, blue running into grays, making a color so clean it didn't compare to anything he knew. At that moment, he was eternally grateful that she couldn't see him as well as she should.

"Can I ask you something?" she said.

He would have given her the world when she looked at him like that. It made him feel warm and alive. "Anything," he answered.

"Would you please get naked, too?"

Laughing, he complied in record time. And then he lay down next to her.

The lights were low, the air filled with the cool breeze from the air conditioner, but his body was tense, his blood hot and full of anticipation.

There was no more waiting.

Finally, he could touch her.

Carefully he found the thin white scar that traversed her abdomen and pressed his mouth against it. "Very sexy," he said.

"Thank you," she said politely, amazingly prim for a woman who was wearing no clothes.

He used his hands to explore her, watching her face as he learned what pleased her. She bit her lip when he lingered at the bend in her arm, when he traced the curve behind her ear and when he stroked her breast.

Unable to resist, he drew her nipple into his mouth, her body jumping in shock. He pulled her closer against him and began to suck. Her legs moved restlessly, fighting the power inside her, but he didn't want her to fight it, he wanted her to let go. He covered her with his body, trapping her legs between his own and then refocused his attention on her other breast.

This time her hips rocked against him, her pelvis curling and uncurling with such finesse, he had to pull back.

"Honey, you're going to have to slow down," he

said. He knew they weren't going to be together forever. With her brains, it'd only take one night for her to
see the mistake she was making, and he was determined that everything be perfect so he could remember
it forever.

However, he had underestimated Michelle. She
laughed, and Miss Prim and Demure disappeared. She
rolled against him, her hand reaching down to boldly
stroke him.

Holy Mary. Quickly he bracketed both of her hands
in his and pulled them above her head.

"Stay there," he ordered.

"Like this?" she asked, grabbing the iron rails of the
headboard and arching her back, which caused him a
small heart attack. Michelle Cushing Coleman was not
only brainy, but a minx. It was enough to make a lesser
man run.

Just to punish her, he went back to all the places that
had made her moan before. He kissed with his lips, he
nipped with his teeth, he delighted her with his tongue.
Each time her hands fell from the rails, he replaced
them, tracing the soft line of her arm with his lips, then
ending with one soft bite. Because she'd been bad.

As her eyes grew wilder, he worked his way in a line
down her legs. Such perfect legs. Long, lean, but full of
power. Each part held his attention. He discovered she
was ticklish on the back of her ankle; he found a sensi-
tive spot on the back of her knee and slowly, carefully,
he parted her thighs.

Her hips arched upward, but this time he was prepared.

He put one finger inside her, testing, finding her beautifully damp. "Very, very nice."

He put his mouth to the soft mound and began to tease her, putting aside his own needs, wanting to pleasure her. She would never realize what she'd given him, and he had to do something for her.

Her small gasps of air told him exactly what she liked, and he returned again and again until her breathing became ragged and her hands locked in his hair. When her body bucked beneath him, his muscles shook, a warning that he was losing it.

Quickly he sheathed himself and in one hard thrust, he was inside her.

*Oh.*

She was tight and wet, and her legs wrapped around him, locking them together.

One night, just one night.

For three heartbeats he closed his eyes, feeling the blood pulse through his body. The heated air was heavy with her spicy scent and the distinctive smell of sex. Neither of them moved.

Eventually he gathered his control and he kissed her, counting each kiss in his head, knowing it wasn't enough. She tasted of mint—marvelous, mundane mint.

Then he began to thrust, slowly at first until they were moving in rhythm. Her eyes never left his, the trust never disappearing. There was something deeper that lurked in the blue depths, something that made his hand reach for hers and clutch desperately.

Then he forgot to think, forgot to count, simply pounded into her until they were one.

# 8

*ONE NIGHT.*

Mickey heard the soft whisper in her ear and she wanted to cry. Minutes ran into hours, time moving much too quickly. Her kisses became more frantic as the night grew darker. He never stopped touching her, never stopped kissing her.

Pleasure and pain merged together as her body tired. Still she welcomed him to her.

*One night.*

His back was slippery to her touch, but her hands held him tightly. Each time her fingers slipped, she went back, and this time held him tighter.

Some part of her understood the reasons why. Some part of her even agreed. But her heart cried.

She had finally found someone that she could love. And sex would be all she could have. But she didn't care. She kissed him desperately, angrily. While he thrust inside her, their bodies quietly in tune in ways their worlds would never be, she buried her lips against his neck. Furiously she sucked at the warm flesh, marking him in her own way. The movement kept her mouth sealed, kept her from saying words that she shouldn't.

Stupid words.

So she kissed his mouth, his neck, the scar on his arm. Anything to keep her silent.

The covers wedged in between them, and angrily she kicked them away. Tonight was for her. It was all she had.

Finally, when the first light was breaking along the wall, they fell asleep together, arms and legs entangled.

The night was over.

MICKEY AWOKE AN HOUR LATER, savoring the sound of Dominic's even breathing. Her eyes felt tired and dry, and every muscle in her body was sore. Slowly, she stretched, pieces of her aching in places she'd never known existed.

She, who never called in sick, thought about calling in sick, but what would that solve? Dominic would be gone soon. No reason to laze about in bed.

She watched him sleep, his features softened and gentled in repose. What things had he done in his life? She wanted to ask, but didn't dare. As her father had often said, some truths were better left unsaid.

And wouldn't he have a fit if he knew? Mickey had never been rebellious or flighty. She was intelligent, ambitious and focused. Just as a Coleman should be. Hell, she didn't even know that she had it in her to do something so unconscionable as to actually sleep with a known criminal.

She told her brain to shut up, but once started, her brain never turned off, and the doubts began bombarding her mind like so many streaming pions.

*What if he had actually killed somebody?* She'd seen the marvelous way he'd handled John. That came from experience, not from theoretical research. And the way he broke in through the window. It didn't look like the first time he'd done that, either.

Yet in his sleep he looked so innocent. She sighed. He was so perfectly made, it was like Apollo had come down from the heavens and slipped into her bed.

It didn't matter what he looked like, or how carefully he listened to her, or how passionately he made love. She wouldn't see him again.

Facts were facts.

There were two categories of men: Fling and Relationship. Flings were the secret ones, the ones that got written up in the diary, but that was about it. Hot sex, no regrets. The badder, the better because that way the line never got muddied. The Relationship men—okay, there'd only been three of those in her life—they were the acceptable ones. Intelligent, loyal and dependable. Guys you brought home to dad.

But a Fling guy would never come charging to her rescue. A Fling guy would never call her exquisite. Heck, even the Relationship guys never called her exquisite. No one had ever done that but Dominic.

Painfully her heart clenched inside her chest. Get over it, Mickey, she reprimanded herself, this is a guy who will end up in jail or swimming with the fishes.

She climbed out of bed and walked to the window, just in time to see the brilliant fireball light up the sky. A new day. Any other day and this would be her favorite time to be alive.

She pushed the lace curtains aside and watched while all the world was still. Her apartment faced a long expanse of parkland, and far off she could hear the traffic from the freeway. But that was another place. Here, in her window, there was only green. Green trees, green grass that was decorated by the patchwork of white trillium that managed to bloom in the summer.

A group of blue grosbeaks squawked angrily. Probably some female, kicking her Fling bird out of the nest. She watched the single bird that was left sitting alone.

Stupid bird.

"I should be leaving."

At the sound of his voice, Mickey turned. He was more than half-dressed, looking in a huge hurry to get out of there. Typical Fling guy. The long hours of making love had disappeared, leaving only the morning-after awkwardness.

Suddenly her nudity seemed out of place and overdone. She walked over to her closet and pulled a wrinkled, oversize T-shirt from the pile of clothes at the bottom. Thank God for closet doors. So easy to throw everything out of sight.

"You should take a plant with you," she said, wanting to fill the empty silence. "You'll breathe better."

She wanted him to have something that was hers. Something that he could look at, and think of her. She wanted to think he would think of her. If he killed it, well, she had recovered from heartbreak before.

He walked over to her, closer, as if he wanted to touch her. She held her breath, wondering if he was going to break the rules. One-night stands didn't involve secondary touching. That implied something more.

He didn't touch her, but his eyes were nice, and a little unsure. "You're really going to give me a plant?"

"If you'd like," she said with a casual shrug.

He smiled. "I'd like."

As she walked into the living room, he followed, and she raised the blinds, flooding the room with the light from the east.

"You know, you should have frosted glass or something. People could see in and know you're here alone. It's dangerous," Dominic said, walking over and testing her door lock.

"You know a lot about safety," she said, raising an eyebrow.

He shrugged. "Comes with the territory. You need to be careful."

Because now there was no one else to look after her. Now she was back on her own. "Thanks," she said, wondering if she should shake his hand.

He shoved his hands into his pockets, no hand shaking there, and waited.

The plant. Oh, God. She grabbed one of her favorite ivies. Seven years old and completely dependable. "This is Persimmon."

"A persimmon plant?"

"No, that's her name."

"Oh," he said, in a tone that spoke volumes. *You're a fruitcake, Mickey.*

Mickey ignored the tone. No one else knew she named her plants, not even Jessica, who knew everything. "Just water her once a week. She can go two weeks if you forget, but she'll get yellow and droopy. If you talk to her, it helps."

Seriously, he nodded. "Okay."

And now they were back to goodbye. She put on a perky smile. "Well, thanks for everything."

He clutched the plant to him, a barrier made of clay, dirt and carbon-based life-forms. "Yeah."

"You know how to get back to the city?"

Dominic nodded.

"I should pay you," she said, remembering their agreement.

He looked slightly disgusted. "I'm not taking your money. Forget about it."

Like she could. "See you around," she said, even though she was never going to see him again.

He turned toward the door, opened it and then shut it. "Michelle..."

Her heart started thumping, and she held her breath. Please, please, please.

He took one step closer. She waited.

One more step and then there was only Persimmon between them. "You be careful," he said, his face lined with worry, his eyes tired.

"I'll be fine. I always am," she said, keeping with the perky smile.

He bent his head. He was going to kiss her. That fabulous mouth was going to touch hers once more.

She parted her lips and closed her eyes.

It was soft and careful. So careful she wanted to cry.

She didn't open her eyes when he lifted his head, nor when he opened the door. In fact, it was a good ten seconds after the door closed that she dared to peek.

Once again, she was alone in her apartment.

First thing she needed to do was water the plants. Mechanically she went about her morning routine. Shower, one bowl of cereal and the morning paper. She watched the news and saw all the pain and suffering in the world. Eventually she turned off the television and left for work.

Today was just another day, and if she reminded herself of it often enough, she just might start to believe it.


MICKEY SAYS: "You there?"

Silence.

Mickey says: "You there? Oh, forget it. I'm using the phone."

"Beth?"

"Hello?"

Mickey wasted no time in telling the part she wanted to tell. "I'm in the clear. There never was a tape."

"The cretin!"

Mickey couldn't agree more, but since there was no sign of John nor his possessions in his cubby, she wouldn't be able to tell him in person. Darn.

At Beth's prompting, Mickey gave her the Cliff's Notes version of what happened, omitting that little bit there at the end. That secret was going to her grave.

"Are you going to—"

"We said goodbye," said Mickey in a tone that closed the subject—permanently. "I've been thinking. We all should get together on Saturday. Jessica will be back."

Beth took the hint. "That sounds like fun. Oh, I forgot. It's your turn to be the voice of reason. Benedict O'Malley is back in Chicago. Divorced. Susan let it slip. Should I say something to Cassandra? She's bound to see him."

Mickey poked at the lonely ivy on her desk. So Mickey wasn't the only one getting screwed in her love life. For once she felt sorry for Cassandra. For once she understood. "Old Nick is back, huh? Don't say anything. Maybe we'll get lucky."

"That's what I was thinking, too. Hey listen, I've been doing the Internet dating service. You need to try this. Three dates lined up for next week."

"Nah. I get too much computer stuff during work. I think I'll meet my men the old-fashioned way. Besides, it's dangerous. You need to be careful, Beth. There's a lot of psychos out there."

"You aren't talking about Dominic, are you?"

"No," said Mickey quietly.

"I was hoping—"

Mickey interrupted. "Never mind."

"Mickey, are you okay?"

"Peachy. You?"

"I'm surviving," said Beth.

"Sold any more confessions?"

"One. 'Tales of a Mafia Princess'—"

*Oh, God.* "Beth! You promised."

"It's not about *you*. It's about a girl who visits Italy and gets swept up in La Cosa Nostra. I'd actually started it when Dominic started coming into the store. He just inspires those sorts of fantasies."

Mickey knew just what she meant. "You're starting to scare me, Beth," she said with a half-hearted laugh, because Beth would expect her to say something like that.

"It's about time," was Beth's reply.

FOR DOMINIC, the week passed in a blur. Every morning he went to Dilly's, and then in the afternoon he visited the pool hall over on Division. It was a good place to be seen. He was starting to recognize some faces. Some he thought were soldiers, and some looked like union guys.

He heard the whispers about the new highway construction project, too. No one said much, but Dominic took it in stride. A good cop just needed a little patience.

As an added bonus, the work kept him busy, a needed diversion. One half of him was dying to see Michelle again, the other half knew that it was for the best. Her plant—he refused to call it Persimmon—did okay except for the one day that he overwatered it and ended up pouring a glassful of mud down his kitchen sink.

Twice he picked up the phone to call her, and twice he hung up.

On Thursday, he went back to Starbucks and found his table, making a few calls and reading the morning paper.

An hour later, Frankie lumbered in, getting a decaf nonfat latte and then settling himself in a chair. His face was split by a huge, self-satisfied grin. At least somebody was happy.

"It's either love or money," Dom said. "Considering you're still wearing those five-year-old Hush Puppies on your feet, it must be love."

"You should be a detective, my friend," said Frankie.

Dominic searched for hidden undertones, but there were none. Frankie was making a joke, nothing more.

"The flowers worked?" he asked.

"Like a champ. Five minutes after I confessed, she was bawling on my shoulder. She never wanted to marry the bastard. After I heard some of the stories, I would've knocked him off myself.''

"She's married?" Hastily, Dominic swallowed some juice. "You should stay away from married women, Frankie. They're trouble," he said.

"Nah. I think she's getting a divorce."

Dom didn't believe it; Frankie was being played. He shifted uncomfortably in his chair. "You don't know what she's going to do."

"Yeah, I do. He lays a hand on her again? Boom," Frankie said, with a dark look on his face.

*Ah, geez.* "Who are we talking about?" Dominic asked, praying he was wrong.

"Amber Amarante."

Dominic swore loud enough to turn heads. "Frankie, this is not good."

Thankfully, Frankie looked a little sheepish. "I know, but I love her."

"Couldn't you fall in love with somebody less married?" urged Dom, this time remembering to keep his voice low.

"No."

Dominic was not one to toss around advice to the lovelorn, so he let up. "What are you going to do?"

"I'm going to marry her."

"Bigamy is a Class four felony. That's five to ten in Joliet, and then you're *still* not married to her. Hell." Dom threw up his hands.

"She said she was going to divorce Vinny," he repeated stubbornly.

"Frankie, I like you, and I don't want to see you dead. Stay away from her."

"I need your help."

Oh, God. It gets worse. "Don't ask me to do this."

"She likes your girl, Michelle. You know Amber isn't used to anybody listening. Vinny just shuts her out. I want her to see how a normal couple works. I want the four of us to go out."

"I will not do this," he said, even while he remembered the feel of Michelle in his arms.

"There's this ghost cruise on the Chicago River; some goombah is holding a scholarship fund-raiser for underprivileged kids. I can come with you and Michelle, and who could guess? We accidentally bump into her. We got it all planned."

"I can't do this, Frankie," Dominic said. One last plea because he had tried to do right by Michelle. He had walked away from her. It was the hardest thing he'd done in his life, and he couldn't do it twice.

Frankie steepled his fingers together, always a bad sign. "Tell you what. I'll give you two points of my action. Tax-free cigarettes. It's a sweet, sweet deal. Consider it my way of returning the favor."

Slowly Dominic lifted his head. It wasn't the way he wanted it, or the way he had it planned, but that's the way it was. "I'll help you, but no Michelle. We split up."

"Well, unsplit up then. Amber liked her. Ergo, I like her."

"I can't, Frankie."

"Oh, come on. Did you screw around on her and now she's not talking? Fix it. I've seen you with the ladies. One smile and they're eating out of your hand."

"I can't fix it," said Dominic tightly. He could still taste her, smell her; it was making him nuts.

Frankie jumped to his feet, faster than Dominic would have thought possible. "Have a good life, Corlucci."

Dominic slammed his hand on the table. This was not supposed to happen. This time he was trying to do the right thing. He couldn't let anything happen to her. Frankie turned and waited.

Sure, and then he'd blow the whole case. So why was he a cop? Why even try?

*Admit it, Dominic, you're a failure.*

He found the medal against his neck and closed his eyes until he found his strength. He could protect her. This time it would work. When he opened his eyes, he knew he was doing right. As long as he did right, it'd be okay.

"I'll do it," he answered.

Immediately, Frankie broke into a broad grin. "I knew I could count on you, Dom."

"Yeah. Dependable Dom. That's me."

JESSICA'S HOMECOMING became a fully baked plan. The girls figured that one day of after-honeymoonage would be plenty. After that, everything should revert to normal. Mickey wasn't sure, because Jessica, who was never a call screener, had let her voice mail kick in all four times that Mickey had called. Mickey tried not to be offended, but the truth was out there.

In deference to Jessica's new nonsingle state, they opted to meet at Mickey's apartment instead of a bar. It was a nice gesture.

After Jessica arrived, Mickey was ready with the first toast. She lifted her martini glass.

"To good men and the one woman lucky enough to find him."

Jessica put down her glass. "That is such a deep pile, Mick. There are lots of great men out there. You just have to meet them."

Beth handed over her olive to Jessica. "Obviously you have forgotten the misery of the search."

Cassandra took a sip of her drink, and leaned back into the couch. "Monogamous sex will kill brain cells. It was a factoid on CNN."

Jessica drained her glass. "Do you want to hear about Tibet?"

"No," they all shot back at once.

Jessica sneezed. "Just asking. So what's happened since I've been gone?"

Beth shot Mickey one of those looks. Mickey gave her a "don't say anything" look back.

However, eagle-eye Barnes, uh, Taylor, spotted it. "What's up?"

At that moment, the doorbell rang and Mickey jumped up. "Whoa! Better run to get that. Might be pizza."

She opened the door on Dominic.

*Not a pizza after all.*

Quickly, she slipped out to the hallway and shut the door behind her, determined not to let him get away and equally determined to hide him from her friends, who just wouldn't understand. "Hi," she said, just like a moron.

"This is a bad time. I knew I should have called," he said. "Look, I'll see you later."

"No!" She grabbed him by the back of his shirt and then, appalled at herself, let go. "I've got some old friends inside and I—" Oh, God, how to explain this without sounding like a snobby bitch?

"It's okay," he said, grabbing her hand. "I understand that part. It's easier this way."

His thumb rubbed against her palm, making it difficult to move. "Thank you," she managed, because at the very least, she should be polite.

"How you doin'?" he asked, his dark eyes cutting right to her heart.

"I missed you," she said, sounding girlie and needy and all those things she despised.

"I missed you, too," he said and then he was kissing her. It felt like three years since the last time he had kissed her, and she put everything into her response. For a moment it was heaven, and then all too quickly he was moving away.

"I'm sorry," he said.

"Do *not* apologize," she snapped.

"I'm so—" and then stopped at her glare. "That's a lie. I'm not sorry at all."

When he looked at her like that, she could have stayed out in the hallway forever. But the neighbors would talk, and eventually her friends were going to try and leave. Surely this was a good sign, though. He had actually come to see her. She flashed an apologetic smile. "I'm not great in the hostess department, but I'm going to have to go inside soon. They'll start looking."

"Yeah. I know. Listen, I didn't want to do this, but I

don't have a choice. I need to ask you out." He groaned, and then rubbed his eyes. "Geez, that sounded like crap. Let me start over. I've been dying to see you again, but I know it's the wrong thing to do, but I'm in need of your assistance. It's about Amber."

"Is she all right?" Mickey asked quietly.

"Yeah, she's fine. Remember Frankie?"

"Big guy, big nose?"

Dominic smiled. "Yeah, that's him. He's trying to talk her into leaving Vinny—I can't believe I'm getting involved in all this—and he wants us to go out with them. On a date. You know, show her life on the outside."

Calmly, he was aiding and abetting in an affair, and she felt shocked. It amazed her to realize how immorally inept she was. "Won't Vinny get mad?" she asked, because Vinny looked like that sort of person.

"He won't know," Dominic said, brushing it aside. "It's some do-gooder thing for a scholarship fund, and she's going to meet up with us. Vinny asked a bunch of people to go. It'll all look legit."

This was her chance to do something. She'd felt helpless about Amber's situation, and hopefully Frankie wasn't the fire to Vinny's frying pan. Frankie didn't look the type; he had this large Pooh-bear thing going on. But the best thing of all, she'd have a perfect excuse to see Dominic again. Because it was an act of charity. It sounded noble—even brave.

Dominic got this resigned look on his face. "It's okay. I know it was stupid—"

"I'd be glad to help."

"No. You know what? Screw Frankie. Forget about it.

You want to go out, we'll do something normal. Movie, dinner."

"No, I want to help," she said, knowing that Amber was the perfect rationalization for doing something that was, once again, incredibly stupid.

"Michelle..." he said, in that husky voice.

She wouldn't let him finish. "You asked. I said 'yes.' Now let's move on."

He studied her, then apparently she passed some test, because he nodded. "If you do this, there's some rules you gotta follow."

"I'm a good rule-follower."

"You can't use your real name. Michelle Jones. Never give out your real name."

"I can do that," she said, thinking it sounded like a damned good idea.

"And we go in my car. Yours stands out."

"Do I have to wear the wig?" she asked, hoping for a *no.*

He started to consider it, but she made a command decision. "No wig. I hate that wig," she said.

"Wear the wig. No arguments. Don't talk much about yourself. Keep everything vague."

"You know, you keep this up, and I'm going to get a complex."

"I don't want you to get hurt. Frankie's a good guy and all—"

"'S all right. I understand."

He promised to pick her up the next night, and then it was time for goodbye.

The door opened and Jessica started to poke her head through. Dominic dodged to the side and Mickey slammed the door in Jessica's face. "Encyclopedia sales-man. You know I'm a sucker. I'll be inside in a minute," she called against the closed doorway.

Dominic snickered. "Encyclopedia salesman?"

Mickey flushed. "Whatever."

"I'll go then. See you tomorrow."

He started to go and then turned back. "One kiss," he whispered and then he was kissing her.

"I could get used to this," she murmured against his mouth.

"I already have," he said, kissing her again.

# 9

AFTER DOMINIC WAS GONE, Mickey had slipped back inside. She *thought* she was in the clear. In fact, they let her slide for two hours, but then Jessica cornered her in the kitchen. "Who was that at the door?"

Mickey pulled out a new bag of chips and poured them into a bowl. "I told you. Encyclopedia salesman."

"Liar, liar."

"Leave it alone, Jess."

She shrugged, popped a chip into her mouth. "Your call. I'm here, but if it's Mr. Intern, I won't hold it against you just because he's five years younger. It's got a certain cachet."

"It's not John."

Jessica studied her, and Mickey waited for the Spanish Inquisition. Nothing. Finally Jessica nodded. "All right. But IM if you need anything."

"I will," answered Mickey, knowing she never would. Some secrets were best kept from people who would not hesitate to tell you how stupid you were being.

"Best friends?" asked Jessica.

Mickey gave her an awkward hug. "Always."

AROUND MIDNIGHT Cassandra and Jessica left, but Beth hung back. "Was that John?" she asked. "I thought you got the tape back."

Mickey had glossed over many details of the night she got the tape back, including the fact that she had made love with one Dominic Corlucci, mafioso extraordinaire.

"I had to pay Dominic. You know those mob types, never get in debt," she said with a laugh.

Beth didn't look like she was buying it any more than Jessica. "Be careful."

"Don't worry," said Mickey with a faux smile. She was getting good at lying to her friends.

When she closed the door, she was all alone. And then she began to smile. Tomorrow. If she could break the time-space continuum and blast right into tomorrow, she would. It might have been stupid, but she really couldn't wait.

ON SATURDAY, Dominic worked it so he arrived right on time. Michelle came to the door, looking gorgeous in a midriff-baring top and pants. She had a great midriff. For a moment, he contented himself with ogling her midriff.

"You look great," he said finally, when speech was again possible.

She smiled and opened her mouth to reply just as the phone rang. She held up a "just a minute" finger to Dom and ran over to get it.

"Hello," she said into the receiver.

"Hi, Dad."

*She had a father. Uh-oh.*

"Yeah, I'm doing fine."

"He's giving the lecture next week. I already told him I would be there. Listen, I need to go..."

"Yes, Dad."

"Yes, it's a date."

*She was telling her father that she had a date.*

"He's very nice."

*Nice? Dom considered that for a minute. Maybe.*

"I don't know."

*What does he do? He's a gangster.* He could see why she was answering what she was.

"I don't know."

*Does he have fourteen degrees? Probably not.*

"Probably not."

*See?*

"I'm glad you're okay. I was worried. I'll make us reservations for dinner."

*But not with Dominic.*

"Okay, if you insist. Bye."

After she hung up the phone, she blew a lock of hair out of her eyes. "Sorry," she said.

"No problem," he answered. *I understand why you just lied to your father about me. Hell, I lie to my own father.*

"Let me get a jacket. This may take a while, because I've got to find it first."

"Sure. I'll wait."

The phone rang again. "I'll get that. Hold on," she yelled from the other room.

*Yeah, Dominic. Don't pick up the phone.*

She ran back into the living room and lifted the receiver. "Hi, Cassandra." She smiled apologetically at Dom.

"Oh, wow. That sounds like fun."

"Tonight?"

*So would she lie, or wouldn't she?*

She twirled with the phone cord, and looked the other way. "No, I'm not feeling good."

*And she would.*

She shot a quick look over her shoulder. Another apologetic smile. "Bad headache. I'm going to take some aspirin and lie down."

"It's probably nothing."

"Y'all have fun. Can't wait to hear all about it."

*And, of course, her friends would know nothing about tonight.*

Michelle grabbed her sweater, and he recognized the guilt in her eyes.

*Don't worry. It gets easier after a while.*

"Ready?" she asked.

"Yeah, we better hit the road," he answered.

*Before someone else calls.*


DOMINIC KNEW THE EVENING was doomed when they first reached the ship. A cruise on the hauntings of Chicago. Mayhem, murder, shipwrecks, I see dead people. Yeah, right up his alley. All they needed was Halloween music, and they could have a party.

The "ghost hunter"—a likely story—was seated near the bow, and most of his audience was listening with rapt attention. He was talking about the capsizing of the Eastland in 1915, and Dom immediately began to wonder if their own ship was seaworthy. Hell, they hadn't even left the dock.

Not that he was superstitious or anything, but still he

rubbed his medal for luck. A couple of extra Our Fathers wouldn't be too far out of line, either.

Frankie was waving from the top deck, so Dominic steered Michelle up the stairs to the open air. Dominic was relieved that Amber had yet to show. If he had his way, Amber would stay home and be sick or something.

After introductions were made, Frankie made nice and went to fetch a couple of beers and a soda for Dominic. It was the least Frankie could do.

"Nice night," he said, even as the ghost hunter began droning about the Edmund Fitzgerald. So how many ships had sunk in the Great Lakes?

"Perfect night for sailing," answered Michelle with a confident smile, obviously not superstitious about shipwrecks, only stars.

She tossed her hair in the cool night air, and then leaned against the railing, bracing her elbows on the polished brass. For a moment Dominic forgot all about the ghosts.

What was it about her? Maybe because he felt like he was starting over. Like somebody had sealed his record.

Sometimes when she looked at him, it just felt like everything was going to turn out okay. He lifted his shoulders and then leaned against the railing next to her.

"Thanks for doing this," he said.

She turned, peering at him over her glasses. "Changed your mind, huh? It's a good thing now?"

"It was always a good thing, just never was a smart thing," he said, and then noticed Frankie approaching, with Amber in tow. "Remember what I told you," Dominic whispered.

"Look who I ran into?" Frankie said loudly, just so the people in Wisconsin could hear, as well. Frankie handed out the beers with all the elegance of a wine steward—an amazing transformation.

Amber talked, chatting about her new hair stylist, and Frankie listened, taking in every word with the absolute goofiest expression on his face. The guy was in love. Definitely. Amber shivered when the guide talked about the monster in the lake, and Dominic poked Frankie in the ribs. That was the general cue for Frankie to play he-man.

Michelle caught his arm. "She's married. You really shouldn't encourage that."

Like he didn't know that, either. "I'm not gunning for him to jump her on board. I just want her to leave Vinny in such a manner that Vinny don't get pissed off."

When Amber turned to talk to some other soldier types, Frankie turned and shot them both a dirty look. "You're not helping here. Look lovey-dovey. Some of that eyeball gazing and shit."

"You want to tell me what to do?" Dominic shot back. "I don't think so." At least Frankie left them alone after that.

Michelle rolled her eyes. "Mr. Romantic, aren't you?"

"No. Not by any stretch of the imagination," he said, defending his right to be whatever he wanted.

"I don't know what my problem is," she said sadly. "I should be all for this. She *needs* to leave the jerk."

Unfortunately, Dominic knew exactly what her problem was. She was used to a world that was evenly divided into right and wrong. Dominic's line of vision had never been that clear.

For the past ten years he'd stayed out of trouble, but things still felt wrong. He still felt responsible, still felt the guilt, and it didn't matter how much he prayed or how many good things he did, it just didn't go away.

He put an arm around her, fitted her under his shoulder, and for a while they stayed there like that, two lovers looking up at the stars.

Frankie pulled him aside and slipped him an address for the cigarettes. One step at a time. The guys at the precinct were going to be proud.

"You want me to put up some cash?" asked Dominic.

"Nah. I trust you. Wait until you unload the stuff, then come see me."

Dominic held out his hand. "I appreciate this, Frankie."

"No problem," he replied, shaking his hand, sealing the deal. "Amber's great, isn't she?"

"Yeah." Dominic glanced around and saw Michelle pointing up at the sky looking scholarly. Time to get back before Michelle was the one they pegged for a cop.

MICKEY HAD SPENT the time pointing out Canes Venatici and Coma Berenices to Amber, showing how to find them in relation to the Big Dipper. Amber was a natural for astronomy, and when Dominic returned, Mickey just kept talking.

She launched into the controversy of the positioning of the constellation, the Black-eye galaxy, and explained how if you looked at it with a four-inch aperture lens or better, it would wink.

Amber seemed completely fascinated, and even Frankie looked a little intrigued.

Suddenly, Dominic grabbed her arm. "Excuse us for a moment," he said, talking to Frankie. "We're going to have a little private time."

Michelle raised her eyebrows at such high-handed treatment, but was willing to give him the benefit of the doubt. He dragged her down to a dark corner on the lower deck, and her insides started fluttering in anticipation. Unfortunately, he didn't touch her, just started pacing back and forth like an electromagnetic wave.

Her insides stopped the flutter.

"You doing okay?" he asked.

She rubbed her arm, which really didn't hurt, but she wanted him to experience guilt since they were not down there for an illicit rendezvous, which is what she had secretly hoped. "I was doing fine, until you contracted an extreme case of *leavus alonus*."

Dominic winced. "Sorry about that. Just being careful."

It was a very nice thing to say, and she appreciated his concern, but she'd really been looking forward to that illicit business. As he was used to crossing over lines, she'd kind of expected it from him. "You know, there is such a thing as *too* careful."

"No, there's not."

Mickey elected not to argue a subjective point. "Frankie's nice. He really likes her."

"Good," said Dominic, looking completely distracted.

"I thought you wanted him to be happy."

"I do. I just got the willies tonight."

"It's all that ghost talk, huh? Too many dead people?"

"Yeah, that's what it is. Too many dead people."

Mickey had her own suspicions. She'd seen him talking to the skinny kid, who looked like he wasn't old enough to drink, much less hook up with the mob. Still, this was none of her business, and the only way a relationship with Dominic would survive was strategic avoidance.

*Is that what they had? A relationship?*

No, she cautioned her brain. Two dates and a long night of unforgettable sex did not a relationship make.

Hot, steamy, thigh-quivering sex...

The fluttering started all over again.

He rubbed the spot on her arm. "I'm sorry. I wish I was better company tonight. Is Frankie bothering you, or anything?"

"No."

"Any of the other guys?"

"No, they've all been very nice. I did get one death threat—"

"What?"

"That was a joke."

He held up a warning finger. "No joking."

Mickey looked suitably chastised. "Right. Rule number three—No joking."

He stopped rubbing her arm and started pacing again. "Want another drink? Something to eat?"

"Dominic, relax."

"Yeah, so—" he started to speak and then leaned back against the railing. His fingers began to drum, and she could just make out the beat to the *William Tell Overture.*

This couldn't be a good sign. "Are you always this nervous? I mean, isn't this just a day in the life here?" she asked, not wanting to pry, but just wanting him to calm down.

"I don't like you seeing this," he stated flatly.

Oh. They were back to the career-choice issues. Mickey didn't want to talk about it anymore. If they ignored it, it might go away. She didn't want to talk at all. She wanted to erase the lines of worry that marred his forehead. She wanted to put the devil's persuasion back into his eyes.

Now was the time to be bold. She locked her arms around his back and planted a good one on him.

At first she felt the tension in him, the muscles bunched tightly under her hands, but this was one battle she could win.

That's what happened when you had one, extraordinarily long night of great sex with a nonrelationship guy—you knew what he liked.

Using her mouth, she pulled on his lower lip, sucking until she felt the muscles begin to relax.

*There you go.*

His hands curled around her, cupping her butt and locking her against him.

Yep, he was thrilled. That was no roll of quarters against her thigh.

She shivered, and his hands stole under her shirt, clenching and unclenching against her bare skin.

Then his mouth caressed the side of her neck, and she

could feel the strong line of his jaw. He had shaved for her.

"You interested in ghost stories?" he asked, whispering in her ear.

"Nah, they're just dead people," she whispered back, letting her hands skim beneath his shirt.

"We should really go upstairs," he whispered, his lips tickling her neck.

"We don't have to," she whispered, thinking naughty thoughts.

He laughed, low and wicked, and she knew he was right on her wavelength. "We're stuck on a boat for two hours, there's seventy-five people milling around. It's impossible."

Mickey walked her fingers up and down his spine. "Nothing is impossible."

His eyes fired to a smoldering black and his grin faded. This was Dominic at his most dangerous.

"Follow me," he said, and she would have willingly followed him anywhere.

They walked down the narrow deck until he found a locked doorway.

"Damn," she said, getting into the true spirit of illicit rendezvous.

"What's a lock?" he asked, and in less than sixty seconds, they were inside.

It was a storage area, stuffed with life preservers and crates of supplies. Not the most romantic of spots, but they could be alone. The deck lights filtered into the room, giving it a nice glow.

When the door clicked shut, the room turned black.

Her eyes couldn't adjust to the dark because there was no light at all, but her other senses took over.

Under her feet, the ship listed back and forth, the sound of the engine a rhythmic constant. Just above the tangy lake air, she could smell the sharp scent of his cologne.

And somewhere he was nearby, because she could feel him. Her skin felt hot and too tight for her body, and the soft cotton became unbearable against her nipples.

Suddenly his hands were tugging at the knot in her shirt and she realized that there was a certain freedom in loving blind. He could be her dream lover—the man who could make her whimper with merely a touch. The man who could possess her soul, as well as her heart.

Unerringly he slid the material off her shoulders. He had memorized her body just as she had memorized his. Then his mouth was on her breast, strong and insistent, and she found herself gasping for air.

Waves of heat pulsed over her, her hands pulled at his hair, needing something to anchor her. He bent her back across one of the crates and used his teeth to nip at her belly.

The room began to spin. Sensation after sensation washed over her, and she could feel her climax approaching.

She said his name, focused on his name, because she was going insane. It was like someone else had stepped into her dream and taken over.

His hands fumbled at her zipper, and he shoved her pants down to her ankles. Carelessly she kicked them aside. There were more important things to worry about. She needed him inside her, and she told him so, over and over again.

As he stood over her, he pressed her back farther against the crate until her back was resting against the hard wood. Then he grasped her ankles and roughly parted her legs. And finally he was inside her.

There was a desperate moment when she adjusted to his size and his muttered "sorry" indicated he knew about her discomfort. But then he was lifting her legs higher and higher until they rested on his shoulders, and she felt like she was being torn apart.

This wasn't going to work. She was a physicist; she knew it wasn't going to work.

He pulled out and slowly thrust in, and she began to reconsider.

Then he did it again.

Yes, it definitely would work.

They moved together, finding the right rhythm, starting slow until her body had opened to him, and then he began to thrust faster.

This was the Dominic Corlucci that she was afraid of. The man who cut deeply to her core and took what he wanted.

If tonight was simply about pleasure, she would take hers, as well.

Her legs locked around his shoulders and she closed off her mind, drifting into the warm waters to simply feel.

Then his hand slipped between their bodies and touched her. At first, it was a light touch. Nothing more than a butterfly. Instinctively her hips curled up against his hand.

"There?" he asked.

"That's good," she said, her teeth clenched, trying to stifle her moan.

"More?" he asked, his finger still flicking lightly against her.

She closed her eyes. She really couldn't keep this inside her. It was like being trapped inside the accelerator, watching the particles spin around and around, flying through the air.

Their moist skin slapped together, the sound echoing inside her head. The hard wood was cutting into her back, dear God, she'd never been so completely pulled inside out, but all she could feel was him. It was rough and sweaty and so completely alive. With each stroke, he was pushing farther inside her, higher and higher...

In the dark, she could hear his strained breathing, the backs of her thighs rising and falling against his chest.

Her hands pulled at the air, trying to find anything to hold on to, anything to keep her sane, but there was nothing. She was completely at his mercy, and Mickey had never been completely at any man's mercy.

Oh, no.

The pressure grew, and he showed no signs of slowing, tilting her legs higher still, until their bodies joined at her heart.

She was going to scream, she was going to scream, she was going to scream.

"You can't scream, Michelle. Here, bite," he said, and he cupped his hand against her mouth. The acceleration was killing her, fourteen Gs pulling her apart and she couldn't survive anymore. She bit, and bit hard, and he pounded inside her again and again.

Finally, he lifted her legs, his cock deep inside her, and he froze. She heard his deep growl, felt his muscles shake with his release, and gently, ever so gently, he let her legs fall back to earth.

She lay there, pretty well dead, and knew that never, ever, would she feel this completely exposed again. Was it just sex? Was this the extraordinary two-night stand? Was it because they were in a boat, with people milling above, doing the impossible?

Sure, she told herself. You've just never been with a man so skilled in the sensual arts. You're just being naive.

He collapsed next to her, not close enough to touch her, but close enough that she felt his warmth calling to her.

It was just sex, she kept reminding herself.

She heard his movements, heard his labored breathing, but he wasn't saying a word.

Then she felt his mouth softly kiss her shoulder.

She grew still, all her nerve endings converging on that one small spot.

A warm shiver danced down her spine, and she wanted to believe it was because of the ghost stories. One small problem—Mickey had never believed in ghosts.

# 10

THE VOICES IN HIS HEAD were getting louder, and Dominic realized that there were people outside the hallway. They were safe here, though; the door was locked, and barring a marine emergency, nobody else was barging in, but they did need to be getting back.

He felt around for clothes, found Michelle's breast, explored for a moment, and then berated himself for getting distracted again. That's what the problem was—she was a first-class distracter, and just when he really couldn't afford to be distracted.

He found her shirt and handed it in her general direction, not really knowing what to say.

He was smart enough to know that he wasn't supposed to tell her he'd just had the best sex of his life. He was smart enough to keep his mouth shut during that critical postcoital phase when either you declared your love or you talked about the next time you were going to see her—whether you meant it or not. With Michelle, he couldn't do either.

The truth was, he wasn't about to analyze his feelings for her, and he wasn't about to ask her out again. She wasn't a cop, she wasn't a criminal, she didn't belong. Period. End of story.

"I think I'm presentable, but I'm not sure my shirt's on right."

Grateful for casual conversation, he latched onto the new issue. "Hold on, I'll crack the door, and let some light in here," he answered, and lifted the handle, prepared to sneak out.

"I don't know what to do, Frankie."

*And close.*

Quietly he leaned back against the door until it clicked shut. Wonderful. They were stuck. And he could have really used a glass of water or anything, because he wanted to avoid conversation right now. And he really needed to be un-alone with her, because every time they were alone, they ended up having sex. And sex with Michelle Cushing Coleman was bad.

Heart-pounding, stomach-wrenching, head-exploding bad. So bad that he was already thinking about doing it again.

*Get your head out of the gutter, Corlucci.*

"We've got company," he whispered in the general direction of her, and took one extra sniff because he really liked the way she smelled. Just like sex.

His body immediately got hard.

"Amber, you can't stay with him. Vinny is one of those guys that just doesn't quit. He's going to keep going and going and eventually there'll be nothing left of you. You're too nice to just disappear into a shell."

"He had Johnny C. killed. I can't believe he had him killed."

Dominic froze. He should've been wired tonight. But wires were risky, and it never would have gotten past Michelle.

"We didn't know that for sure."

"I heard him. He's never had anybody killed before. There are some things I can handle—larceny, extortion, even arson can be made passable. But whacking a living, breathing human being? No. I've got my lines that can't be crossed."

"All the more reason to get out of his hair. I can give you money for a ticket for Miami if you want to start over somewhere new."

"Isn't that nice of you, playing my own personal St. Frank, but I'm not going to start off in a city where I don't have any friends, or don't have a job."

"Let me help you, then."

"You're a good man, Frankie. But you stay out of this one. Promise me. I'll clean it up. I just need to think. My ma always said I was a slow thinker. Like to weigh my options and such."

"Don't wait too long, Amber."

"Nah. I won't. Where do you think Dominic and Michelle went?"

"You need two guesses?"

Dominic winced and wondered what Michelle was thinking. She was being awfully quiet.

"He's a nice man, too."

"Yeah, I think so. Vinny doesn't trust him as far as he can throw him, but I do. I tell him that he's legit, but Vinny doesn't believe him. What does Vinny know anyway? The guy's a joker for not treating you right. If you need anything, and can't get to me, you go to Dom, okay?"

Footsteps echoed on the wood and the voices began to fade, and Dominic blew out a breath.

"Is the coast clear?" she whispered.

He cracked open the door and peeked.

The deck was empty, and he opened the door fully. Michelle stepped outside.

"Ready to go above deck?" he asked, not really in the mood for more haunted stuff, but at least he could think. And he really needed to think.

She didn't answer, and he took another look. Her face was pale in the moonlight, her jaw locked tightly. She was scared.

Cripes, Corlucci, she wasn't used to this.

Awkwardly he patted her arm, but she was still frozen. "Michelle?" he asked, and she turned to look at him.

The look in her eyes was his undoing. Ignoring all common sense, he took her in his arms and simply held her. "I'm sorry," he said, over and over again.

"I didn't realize..." she whispered.

That was easy to do. He'd been so caught up in being with her that he'd forgotten exactly who he was involved with.

Mistake number one. You get careless and accidents follow. He seemed to have trouble with that basic concept.

Dominic pulled back and took her face in his hands. "Hey, just a few more minutes and we'll be off this ship and I'll take you right back home. Just stay with me a little bit longer."

Her eyes refocused and she gave him a small smile. "I'll be fine."

Which was good, because he wasn't. Deep inside him, he knew he'd never be fine again.

THEY DOCKED RIGHT after midnight, and Mickey had never been happier to see dry land. She had been riding on a boat with men who now brokered life and death like a commodity.

*Even Dominic.*

No matter how she tried to ignore the truth, it didn't go away.

It wasn't a TV movie anymore, or a funny story in a confession magazine. She wanted to run, but she didn't. Wasn't this their last night together? Oh, yeah, right. She'd already used that excuse the last time.

Michelle kept between Dominic and Frankie as they disembarked, while Amber had gone on ahead, chatting with some other wives, like it was a typical social club. The couple had remained discreetly apart for most of the cruise, although if Frankie wasn't careful, his eyes would give him away.

How could you not notice when a guy's eyes ate you up? When he looked at you like the entire cosmos—all the galaxies, comets and stars—were bottled in your eyes?

Mickey just wasn't that strong.

A driver pulled up to the curb, and Amber was whisked away into the waiting black sedan. Mickey felt relieved. That probably meant she was a bad person, but danger made her nauseous.

Frankie stopped on the wooden dock, his big body frozen, watching as Amber was driven back to her husband. Mickey's relief was Frankie's pain.

"You all right?" Dominic asked Frankie.

Frankie grunted, an affirmative sort of grunt, but his

hands began to shake. Not a good sign for a man that didn't seem to have a nervous disorder.

Around them, the crowd started to disperse, everyone making their way home. "Would you like a drink?" asked Michelle. Frankie was starting to worry her with his hand-shaking.

He grunted again. Such a typical guy.

"We gotta go," Dominic said casually, as if Frankie sounded completely lucid. "If you want to talk or anything, just call. Don't do anything stupid, huh?"

Then Frankie walked alone to his car, his shoulders slumping low. Michelle felt a surge of pity for the big guy. He was headed for a heartache. As they watched, he drove away, a flash of red taillights squealing into the darkness.

"Is he going to be okay?" asked Mickey.

"He'll survive," Dominic said in a flat voice. "I'll take you home."

Home. Schaumburg sounded wonderful. Her plants, her television, day-old pizza. And Dominic would be in her home, as well.

Instead of being scared, or planning her escape route, she just wanted to climb into a comfortable T-shirt and settle on the couch with him. He could hold her, like he'd done before, and keep her safe.

A little wide-eyed moment from a woman who was a card-carrying realist, but she needed to hang on to something.

The water lapped gently against the docks, and high above, Virgo was watching over the world. It was a beautiful night, a night for lovers.

He grabbed her hand, his skin warm and comforting.

At that moment, Mickey just wanted to live, because tomorrow he would be gone.

When they got to her building, Dominic walked her to the door. "I'm not going to stay or anything, honest. I just want to make sure you get in okay."

There he stood, his hands locked resolutely behind him. Mickey saw the writing on the wall. Not that she hadn't written the same words on that very same wall, but so far she'd been awfully good at ignoring it. He didn't seem to have the same problem. And so the bit of hope that she'd been lugging around inside her took one last little breath and died.

"I'm not going to see you again, am I?" she asked.

He shook his head.

"Okay," she said quietly, not wanting to sound disappointed, but she did.

Things were better this way, and even if it made her scream inside, well, she'd get over it. She'd lived every day just getting over it.

They were strangers—poles, continents, universes apart—yet he'd seen something in her that no one else had. Not her father, not Jessica, not Dr. Romanowski, not anyone. Some particle of femininity, of softness, that she didn't know she possessed. It was their little secret and made the relationship all the more intimate, and all the more dangerous because she liked it.

If only...

When he turned to walk away, she stopped him. "Wait a minute." Her brain worked to find suitable topics of conversation, but nothing emerged. Let him leave, she screamed inside her head.

"I gotta go," he said, avoiding her eyes, but she noticed that he wasn't moving.

"Can I ask you something?" she asked, an insanely stupid question because she had no questions that she would dare ask. She wanted to know if he cared about her, but she'd never actually say the words. They were too wimpy, too angsty, but still, she wanted to know.

"Probably not a good idea," he said, still not looking at her.

"Yeah," said Mickey with a soft sigh. The lack of an answer was an answer itself. Suck it up.

"I'll see you around," was the last thing he said to her.

"Don't get caught," she whispered to herself, and waited until he'd walked out of sight to go inside.

Her apartment was dark, the light on the answering machine blinking like a red eye. She flipped on the single overhead bulb, but the light popped, and darkness fell once more. Only now the darkness that she usually craved was strange. It was the perfect end point to a disappointing night. Everywhere she looked, shadows appeared. New and unfamiliar shadows.

You're just freaked out, she thought to herself. All those eerie stories. You're just seeing ghosts.

As she carefully crept in the direction of the answering machine, she listened to the silence.

Moonlight drifted between the swaying tree branches outside her window.

She reached out, her fingertips using the back of the couch as her guide. She could hear her own breathing, in and out, in and out, and then another sound joined in. Faint and soft, like someone else's breathing.

You're being silly, she thought. Get over it.

Then she felt it—just a light touch on her arm.

She screamed.

Armed with her purse, she tackled the intruder, pulling him to the floor. A loud crash rang near her head.

The door burst open, and she heard Dominic call her name.

*Thank you, God.*

The lamplight came on, flooding the room.

*Crap.*

She had captured her ficus tree and pulled down a whole shelf of African violets in the process. Dirt covered the living-room floor, and the plants were lying helplessly on their sides.

She had screamed. She, the one who would never consider screaming, had screamed. If there had been no witnesses, she would have beat her head against the wall. Hard. However, Dominic was there to save her from her pain.

He stared at the mess, trying not to laugh, which earned him several brownie points. "I heard you yell."

She stood with as much dignity as possible and began to dust off the clumps of dirt from her clothes. "Just being clumsy," she said.

"I thought something was wrong."

"Oh, no, nothing wrong," she twittered, and righted the tree.

He bent and picked up the other pots off the floor. "I'll help you clean up."

She should have told him to go, then at least she could have had her pride, but she didn't.

So for half an hour, they worked in silence. Mickey

pulled out her Dustbuster and got most of the dirt off the floor. The carpets would have to be shampooed, but that seemed a small price to pay.

"Need something to drink?" she asked. She felt like she should offer him something, and she really wasn't aching for him to stay. She really wasn't.

"No, thanks," he said, but he didn't run for the door.

"Oh." A witty, scintillating, monosyllabic answer if ever she'd heard one.

"You were scared?" he asked, his eyes smiling and her miniuniverse realigned.

Weakness was never tolerated in the Cushing family, so she dipped her head, studying the floor. "Only a little bit."

"I understand."

He collapsed in the chair, looking like he was going to stay. Something warm and sunlike bloomed inside her. He was going to stay.

DOMINIC WATCHED HER settle in the chair, watched the smile widen on her face. They'd just crossed the line. He knew it and so did she. Passion, sex, those things you could walk away from. Intimacy and secrets bonded you together, screwed you in tight.

"Do you get scared?" she asked, her eyes boring into him, searching for his secrets.

"Oh, sure," he said easily.

"Of what?" she asked.

The truth still terrified him. Ten years later and he still lived in the fear that NYPD would track him down and pin him as an accessory to manslaughter. According to the letter of the law, when a felony crime results in a death, all parties can be charged and Dominic was one of those parties. "I don't like lizards," he said, looking her straight in the eye.

She kept going after him. "Don't you get scared that you'll go to prison, or you'll get killed, or cut in half or something?"

At one time, he would have welcomed death. Not anymore. "We're all going to die someday," he answered.

Her hands started to circle in the air, her face so intent. "Yeah, but there's no reason to rush it. I mean, you don't smoke, right?"

"No."

"You use your seat belt when you drive?"

"Yeah."

"And drive the speed limit?"

"Yeah."

"So, you do all these things to extend your lifespan. Why don't you choose a career that might offer a retirement plan? Something in retail. Or the service industry is really hot right now. And health care! Health care is full of opportunities."

"Michelle..." he said, and he knew where this was going. She wanted to see something better in him than there was, but there was nothing there.

She ignored him and barreled on ahead. "And then there's the security business. I bet you could do really well in that."

"Michelle..."

She wasn't going to let him talk. "I could see what we have at Astrophysical Sciences Research Center. You know there's lots of things you could do, depending on your level of experience. Did you go to college?'' she asked.

And she waited. Her clear eyes staring at him, blinking rapidly with something that looked like worry. And suddenly he felt like a selfish pig letting her suffer on his behalf. Well, maybe that was overly dramatic, maybe secretly he wanted to believe that she saw something in him that really did exist. And so he let the first of his secrets slip out.

"I'm a cop."

She didn't notice. "That involves college," she said with a sigh of relief. "That would open up all sorts of career possibilities."

And then it clicked. She smiled, and it was like a million stars were lit in the sky, just for her.

He'd never seen anything more beautiful in his life.

"Thank God."

# 11

DOMINIC KNEW IMMEDIATELY that he shouldn't have told her. He should have let her think the worst of him; it was closer to the truth. But he wasn't going to stop, either.

"I'm undercover, and I'll be undercover for a while," he said immediately, and the softness gave way to curiosity. It was fun to watch her brain work. No wonder she was a scientist.

"Can you talk to me about it? I saw *Serpico*, but that's been a long time ago."

"I shouldn't say much," he answered, but then he went right into telling her about his exploits, about being first in his class at the academy, about the thrill of having a gold shield, even if he couldn't carry it. Things he'd never told anyone before, because it never felt right.

The gates had opened, and tonight he wanted her to know everything that was good about him. He told her about rescuing a dog, he told her about stopping a hijacking, he even told her about the time he was walking home from the station when he busted up a fight between two rival gangs. Everything just poured out in a rush.

Every goddamned good thing he'd done in his life. It

took two hours to cover everything. And he made sure that she knew everything, because he wanted to be good. For ten freaking years he worked to stay on this side of the law, to do the right thing, and tonight was the first time he was glad that he'd done it.

He felt worthy.

"So you're investigating Vinny?"

And back to the present. "I'm not going to say much about the investigation. It's better for you that way."

"But maybe I can help?"

When pigs fly. "I don't think so. It's illegal for cops to involve citizens in an investigation. Code 4763-B," he lied.

"But you helped me with John. Why didn't you tell me to go away?" she asked.

Every day he wondered about that. He had told himself that it was her body, or the sexy way she walked, but not one of those things came close to the truth.

She was smart, sexy and funny, but she found feelings in him that he didn't think he was capable of.

It was the way she looked at him. First she would blink in that "I'm a brainiac" way. Then the trust appeared. The trust did it. It clutched at his gut, and started the pistons churning. When she looked at him like that, he got a hard-on that was currently unmatched in the ongoing saga of Cordano erections. It sounded stupid, and he was never going to tell a soul, so when he smiled at her, it was just a little goofy and he knew it.

"You had great legs," he said.

"That's so cool," she said. "Nobody's ever noticed my legs before."

She went on happily and told him stories about her life, confessed her father didn't understand her and, in general, gave him the rundown on key details of her life in a little under an hour. Just like they'd known each other forever.

He didn't have the heart to stop her. At 3:00 a.m., she finally yawned, and he knew it was time to go. There was lead in his feet, and it took a lot of effort to move them, to do the right thing. He wanted to stay. Goddamn he wanted to stay, but he couldn't do that to her. This was his shot to get out of here. He had to try. This wasn't the time; of course, there really wouldn't be a good time, either.

"Listen, you've had a long day, and everything seems to be okay now," he started.

Her eyes blinked rapidly, all circuits firing. "You don't have to go. I mean, I just assumed. There's no reason that we couldn't—now that you're who you are."

"I have to go," he said flatly, wishing he could just rip out his own tongue.

"Oh," she answered softly. One short syllable that stung worse than any bullet. The blinking stopped. Message received. She faked another yawn. "Yeah, I've got to get up early tomorrow myself.

"See you around, huh?" she said, as she walked him to the door. But it wasn't a question.

"Michelle..." he began.

"Hmm?" she said, with a perky grin pasted on her face.

"If I weren't on this case," he tried to explain.

"That's very nice of you to say, but you don't have to make excuses. I'm not a child."

"It's not an excuse."

"What? Undercover cops can't have a life?"

The short answer to that was no. "It won't work. Vinny and those guys, they know you. Families are kept separate from the case. Majorly separate."

"All right. Goodbye, Dominic," she said, holding open the door.

Now that the exit was staring him in the face, he wasn't ready to leave. He didn't like the way she was staring at him, as if he were something vile. "You don't understand."

"Goodbye, Dominic."

He turned to go. Got one foot out. But he wasn't going anywhere, and damn her for being willing to throw everything away so easily.

"Now let's think about this. It won't work. I would disappear for days at a time. You couldn't call me. What if you needed me for something? You'd be stuck. Hell, I haven't even told you my real name."

She stared at him blandly, all trust gone. He needed it back.

"You'd be miserable," he said, staring her down.

She rose, putting them nose to nose. "I have spent my life working my butt off to get what I want. I've always done things my own way; sometimes I wanted to, and sometimes I didn't have a choice because everyone else around me was screwing up. If you want something, if you really, really want something, you sacrifice. That's the way it works, Mr. Whatever Your Name Is. You, obviously, do not want things badly enough. Goodbye."

He caught the door before she could slam it. "So that's what this is about? You think I'm just dumping you here, because I'm some superficial dirt-wad? You think I don't want this?"

He had her up against the door. "I've never wanted anything more in my entire life, but I'm not going to do it."

"Because it's too dangerous?" she asked in a sissified voice.

"Yes," he said, his hands already settling in. She was familiar and addictive, and he wasn't that strong.

She brushed him off. "Things that are too good to be true always are. Get away from me."

Dominic knew he was missing something big here. She was royally ticked and he didn't understand. "I'm just trying to do the right thing," he said in his own defense.

She shot him a serious "go to hell" look. No blinking at all. "Do I look like I want you to do the right thing?"

"No," he said quietly, the light beginning to dawn.

"Thank you. I am quite capable of making my own decisions. Why don't you ask me if I would like to be in a relationship where you disappear for weeks at a time?"

"Days, not weeks," he muttered.

"Or maybe you should discuss whether the lack of communication is going to bother me?"

Dom ran a hand through his hair. "There are actually ways around that. We just set up a code, that's all. And these guys know you as my girlfriend anyway."

"And now for the big one. Just how mad will I be if I don't know your real name? A lot? Or maybe not at all?" She shrugged.

"It's Cordano. Dominic Salvatore Cordano," he announced, and she looked so pleased that he had a suspicion he'd been played by a master.

"So, does that mean we're going to try this?" she said, her voice soft and vulnerable. The tough talk was over and all his resolve was being eaten away, not to mention his good intentions flying out the door, because he couldn't think around her. She wore the most beautiful smile, he really did love her legs, and the trust was settling back in her eyes.

Dating an undercover cop, loving an undercover cop was hard work, but for the first time, he thought maybe he was worth it.

"If you're up for it," he answered slowly.

"If *I'm* up for it?" she shot back with a sly grin. "Why do you even ask?"

"You can't tell your friends anything," he said, even as he pulled her closer. His hands ran up and down over her, his own private paradise.

"I told you, I'm a great rule-follower."

He kissed her because he had to. She didn't know it, but she'd just given him some piece of himself back. Something he'd tried to find on his own by enforcing the law, by wearing out his knees on a pew, but nothing had worked.

Tonight he was starting over. And all because of her.

"And you can't tell your family. When the case is over, I can do narcotics or vice. It's not so bad. Dime bags and prostitution. It's a walk in the park."

Slowly, she backed him up until he was pinned against the couch. "No prostitution."

"Have I told you that I really love pushy women?"

She didn't let him reply.

MICKEY SLEPT IN the next morning, a new and unfamiliar lump of warmth in her bed.

"Want breakfast?" she asked, finding a hard shoulder. Exploring a hard shoulder.

"I'm not much of a breakfast eater. Maybe coffee?"

Then the phone rang, and Mickey reached over Dominic to pick it up.

"Hello?" she said, collapsing on top of him.

"Mickey, are you alive?" It was Beth.

"Of course. Why shouldn't I be?"

"I left four messages for you last night. I just thought you were comatose or something."

"Oh, yeah. I'm feeling a lot better. Good drugs," she answered, just as a wicked hand crept between her legs. And not her own. She sucked in to breathe.

"Would you be up for some marathon shopping? There's a huge sale at Abercrombie and Fitch. Cassandra's going to meet me there at noon."

"Oh, shopping?" she said, her hips following the magical hand. "You know, ummmmm, maybe tomorrow. I could take off work. Drive into the ah, city."

"You're acting weird, even for you."

"It's all the stress," she answered, even as Dominic slipped inside her.

"You don't want company."

"Not today. Tomorrow. After work."

"Deal. They've got a mango martini. Saw the recipe in *Chicago Woman*. Sounds primo."

"Bye," said Mickey. Then she tried to hang up the phone, but, well, maybe she got a little distracted. Maybe a lot.

IT WAS SOME TIME LATER when Mickey stirred. There was a naked man in her bed. Oh, what a glorious day. "So, how's this going to work?"

Dominic sat up, his chest smooth and rock hard. "We could eat, drink, go see a movie. But I have to say that I'm not a morning person," he said with a serious look.

Like she was going to toss him over because of that. "What amazing karma."

"I like to stay in bed late when I can."

"Yes, your aura seems to say that about you."

"In fact..." he caught her beneath the covers, "I think my aura is growing."

"Again?" she asked, rather pleased. Who knew she was insatiable? It was an aspect of her physical nature that she hadn't known before.

Dominic smiled, the most wonderfully wicked smile. "Honey, we've only just started. I've got a *lot* of time to make up for."

And he did.

IT WAS LATE AFTERNOON when the doorbell rang. Mickey raised her head from the floor.

"That was the doorbell," she stated stupidly. Somewhere between noon and one, she had lost all concept of reality.

Dominic sounded much more lucid. "You should answer that."

Mickey stood and shrugged on her robe. "I'll be back."

When she opened the door, Jessica was there, beaming brightly. "Hey," she said, walking in. Then she gave Mickey a long once-over. "You look like hell."

"Thank you for my daily affirmation."

"How are you feeling?"

"I've been better," answered Mickey, thinking that she'd been better just ten minutes ago when Dominic had been quite happily exploring her breasts with his mouth. Her nipples perked in memory.

Jessica sat down, making herself at home. "Do you need medicine? You're usually very healthy."

"I just need some rest. I think I've been working too hard. It's all catching up to me." She should feel guilty, wanting her very best friend in the world to leave, but her breasts were still perking, saying, "Please, leave." Silently, Mickey told her breasts to behave.

"Oh, my. It's getting deep in here. You, working too hard? Ha!"

Now that stung. "Working too hard is not just a behavioral trait of driven, ambitious people who can't stand not to win," she said, because two could play dirty.

Jessica waved her hand. "It doesn't matter. I need to talk."

"Now?" asked Mickey, as she pulled her robe tighter. Just in case her body was giving off carnal radiation.

"Well, yes. Is there a better time?"

Mickey sat down. "Obviously not. What is it?"

"Oh, I can't tell," said Jessica with a sneeze.

Mickey merely raised an eyebrow. Jessica did not have Mickey's willpower. When she did something stupid, it was just going to come out.

And so, Jessica kept talking. "No. I have to talk to someone about this. Yesterday, I was walking by the Pier, and they're doing some construction. Anyway, there's this great-looking construction-worker type and he whistled."

Mickey waited, but Jessica was just staring at her, like that was the end of the story.

*Because it was the end of the story.* Mickey sighed. "Jessica, men do whistle at attractive females. I've heard that, although only actually experienced it once."

Jessica pulled out a tissue. "But I felt a flash. It felt good. It shouldn't feel good anymore."

Now this was rich. Mickey was going to have to listen to newlywed angst. Yes, because she couldn't talk about the cool stuff in her life.

*I've just had the most astounding, blood-pumping sex in my life. The man is a god, and a cop. And he's nice. And he thinks I'm sexy. Yes, me, Michelle Cushing Coleman. Sexy. Top that.*

But Jessica was her friend—sometimes her only real friend, and she wasn't stupid enough to blow it. "Why shouldn't you feel good? Aren't you human?"

"But it means I'm a failure as a wife."

*He kissed me, J. He kissed me like it's just me and him.* But she couldn't say that.

She rubbed her eyes, playing the part of Mickey Coleman, resident wiseass. "Oh, puh-lease. Jessica, do you love your husband?"

"Well, of course, he's like—Adam. What's not to love?"

"Are you going to have a fling with construction-worker dude?"

"In his dreams," said Jess, with a cocky head toss. Women who looked like J. could do that.

"Have I made my point here? Do you really need me

to tell you how to be married?" If Jessica answered yes, then she was going to pull out her death ray and lobotomize her right there in the chair.

"You're the only person I can tell this to. Cassandra doesn't understand the sacraments of marriage, and Beth—well, I just can't tell Beth."

It was the need to confide that Mickey objected to. She didn't have the luxury to reciprocate, and it was already causing stress levels to rise. "Jessica, now that you're married, you're going to have secrets and you don't have to tell them to me."

"I've always told you everything. We're best friends. It's what we do."

"Do you really want to tell me everything now?" asked Mickey, prepared for the worst, but she knew the drill. Major relationships changed things and secrets were a part of evolution.

Jessica's eyes got big. "No, I can't tell you everything."

"That's because you have new loyalties. Respect your instincts," said Mickey, now playing the part of the wisewoman who knew nanocosms about men.

"You think I'm okay here? I'm not destined for divorce? I don't want a divorce."

"Whistling reception is not grounds for divorce. You're safe. Go home to your husband and treat him to all sorts of fun sexual favors."

*Because as soon as you leave, I'm having fun sexual favors, as well.*

"See, this is why you're my best friend. Cassandra would have me talked into an affair."

"I'm not Cassandra. Not even close," said Mickey, as

if the point needed clarifying, which, of course, it didn't.

"So how are you doing? You're not sleeping well."

Mickey swallowed her bubble of hysterical laughter. She was lucky if she'd gotten three hours of sleep last night and, if there was a God, she'd get even less tonight. The man had a perfect mouth. It was a gift to womankind that no other woman would ever be party to. If they were, she was going to shoot them.

"What?" asked Jessica.

"Someday I'll tell you," said Mickey, savoring the feeling of advantage. It was a rare moment and savorworthy.

"Now you're keeping secrets from me? It's because I'm married, isn't it? You can't relate anymore. Are we going to drift apart and see each other once a year, and then start avoiding saying hello at parties because it's just too embarrassing? And if that happens, who can I dump on? I gotta learn this wife stuff."

"You can read a book," replied Mickey.

"Yeah, I got fourteen the other day at the bookstore. But they are so *not me.* All that woo-woo stuff, and then they're talking about giving each other space. What sort of marriage is that? And then, there was this one, *The Domestic Diva.*" Jessica laughed mockingly. "Can you imagine? Me?"

Mickey listened with half a brain, lost in her own fantasy world. Dominic did that to her. She crossed her legs tightly, pretending he was there.

"How was the honeymoon?" she asked, when Jessica took a breath. She really did want to know. Really.

"Fabulous. We were the first team to the top. Left everybody else in the dust."

"Well, that is what you do best."

And Jessica didn't even laugh. "You're not going to tell me, are you?"

"Tell you what?" asked Mickey, blinking from behind her glasses. It was her best "I know nothing" look.

"Want to go get a drink? I don't have to be home until seven. Adam is working late tonight."

Mickey got up and stretched, inching her way closer to Dominic. "Nah. You go on without me."

Jessica got up and made for the door. "Okay, keep your secrets." After she opened the door, she turned back and wiggled her eyebrows. "But someday you're going to have to explain that hickey on your neck."

Oh, jeez! Mickey clapped her hand over her throat.

Jessica smiled. "Made you look." And then she shut the door.

# 12

THERE WAS SOMETHING narcotic about great sex. It could make you forget ordinary aspects of life. Very important ordinary aspects of life. Mickey never overslept on Monday, but Dominic saved her when he woke up at nine. Then after she got into the office, she had trouble with the data analysis from Dr. Romanowski. Somehow the numbers seemed—well, boring today. And she really needed to finalize the data on her presentation.

Not that she was hugely worried. She'd always been an overachiever, with a capital *OA*. She'd lived and died by the challenge. The presentation would be fabulous. Her father would see her in her native environment. Finally, he would realize that astrophysics was every bit as prestigious as heart surgery. She hadn't exactly saved anybody's life yet, and to be frank, the potential wasn't great, but it certainly wasn't chopped liver, either.

She called him on the phone to tell him, well, actually to brag. She wasn't ready to tell him about Dominic. Not yet, but soon. That is, all she had to say was that he was a truck driver. That couldn't be hard. But she wasn't ready to do it just yet. His personal assistant answered and Mickey left a message.

Messages were the best way to deal with Dad.

Then she went back to work. She ended up staying late because Dr. Fleer wanted a report on a new T-dwarf they had found, and when she finally made it home, it was well after dark. Not so dark that she missed the red rose on her doorstep. He'd left a torn-off cocktail napkin with "From Your Secret Admirer" scrawled on it. Her insides melted into a pile of florally induced goo.

It felt so marvelously free to know she wasn't stupid. She had been right all along. She could trust him. Okay, his job was dangerous. Right up there with lion tamers and cab drivers, but she could live with that. Obviously he was cut from cop-cloth, just like she was cut from star-cloth. She couldn't fault him for following his calling.

She picked up the rose, and took one long sniff of its heady scent. If she worked really hard, she could imagine his scent, as well. Immediately she wanted to go inside and call him. Just to talk. To share the "how was your day?" moments.

In every relationship she'd had before, all three of them, the discussions were based on theories and data. Never once had she had a "Nail any bad guys today?" conversation. There was a great big world out there, and now she was part of it. Dominic's world. She was part of Dominic's world.

Unfortunately, a conversation wasn't possible.

Instead she went inside and called Beth. Not resembling spillage, just chatting. Life was good.

*She was part of Dominic's world.*

ON TUESDAY, DOMINIC got a break. A couple of union guys had met with Vinny at Dilly's. Dominic stayed at the pool tables in the back, shooting the breeze, but he took one quick picture with his cell phone. Gotta love the new technology.

That afternoon, he sent the pictures to the precinct.

Things were moving along. After the cigarette buy, Dominic was accepted. Whoever thought the Outfit was dead didn't know what they were talking about. It was slick and sometimes even legal; these guys had connections.

The wards on the West Side, the laborers' union.

Dominic had time, so he sat back and did what he did best. He listened.

BY WEDNESDAY, Mickey's calm was starting to evaporate. Preparation wasn't her strong suit, and this time "seat of the pants" wasn't going to cut it.

"So, why do you think Monihan disappeared?" Sylvia asked, glancing up from her monitor. "Dr. Romanowski thinks he died, and they're going to break into his apartment, only to find his decomposing body—"

"Can we not talk about that? I really need to find my data file on the star distribution from Rensselar. I swear that I had filed it in this directory. But it's not here."

"Ask Chao. She was poking in your files a few days ago."

"Chao!" yelled Mickey, waving, until she realized she still had her mouse in her hand. Embarrassed, she put it down.

Chao appeared, looking suspiciously guilty.

"Where's the data? *Where is my data?* Do you know what I have left? Three maps and two spectographic charts. And the presentation is," she checked her watch, "seven days, six hours and thirty-seven minutes away."

Chao folded her hands across her chest. "You've been ODing on the coffee again, haven't you? I told you yesterday where your files were. We just needed to find some space on the disk."

Mickey closed her eyes, and found happy thoughts to keep her temper in check. Chao had told her? Not likely. "I'm sure you didn't tell me."

Chao looked unmoved. "Not only did I tell you, I sent you an e-mail, as well. Please check. In this day and age, you can never have too much CYA."

It sounded entirely plausible, although Mickey could swear she had heard nothing. "Well, don't let it happen again," she said, and then stalked back to her computer.

Behind her she heard a murmured, "Who magnetized her Wheaties?"

When she sat down in her chair, rolled on squeaky wheels to the keyboard and checked her inbox, there was the e-mail from Chao. Dated two days ago. Unread. She buried her head in her hands.

*It was the sex.*

Sex was killing her brain cells. The moon-eyed gazing into space, the idle doodling while processing the day's data, it was all because of the sex.

Okay, maybe it was a little more. Maybe she got a little gooey from the way Dominic looked at her, or maybe she drifted off when he rubbed her shoulders while she was watching season three of *Red Dwarf*. How could a woman not fall in love with a man who thought a life-form evolved from a cat was funny?

Immediately she hit the IM session.

Mickey says: "J.?"

Jessica says: "Yo?"

Mickey says: "How did you know when you loved Adam?"

Jessica says: "What is going ON?"

Beth wants to join conversation.

Jessica says: "Okay."

Mickey says, while shrugging in a mysterious manner: "Nothing."

Beth says: "What are y'all doing?"

Jessica says: "Mickey's in love."

Beth says: "OHMYGOD!"

Jessica says, instantly turning to Beth: "What do you know?"

Beth says, putting her hands up: "Nothing. I know nothing."

Mickey says: "Talk and die."

Jessica says, while pounding at the keys in frustration: "Who is he?"

Mickey says: "It's Dominic."

Jessica says, now needing to yell because normal communication channels are failing: "WHO IS DOMINIC?"

Beth says: "Have you thought through all the implications of this relationship?"

Mickey says, while ducking the truth as best she could. "I can't say much."

Jessica says, still pounding at the keys: "Where did you meet him?"

Mickey says innocently: "Starbucks."

Jessica says: "Is he homeless? Unemployed? Why the secrecy? You are not by nature closemouthed."

Mickey says snippily: "Yes, I am by nature close-mouthed. Besides, you were off getting married."

Jessica says, her voice growing even more in intensity: "Oh, yeah, throw that back in my face! You're ducking the truth."

Beth says: "You can't handle the truth."

Jessica says: "That's not funny."

Mickey says: "Actually, it is."

Jessica says: "Answer the #%%#*@ question!"

Mickey says, sticking to her guns: "We met in Starbucks."

Jessica says: "So why did you not tell us about Dominic?"

Beth says smugly: "I knew."

Jessica says: "I want to meet him."

Mickey says, while shifting in her seat. "Give us some time to get through the awkward beginning-dating phase. Meeting friends is a big step toward commitment, and I don't think I'm ready for that yet."

Beth says: "I should hope not."

Jessica says: "Beth, I'm cutting you off unless you tell me what's the issue with Dominic."

Mickey says quickly before Beth can interrupt: "He's a truck driver."

Jessica says: "You're dating a trucker?"

Mickey says: "Yup. Just happened. One of those things."

Jessica says: "And Beth, you've met him?"

Beth says: "Yup."

Jessica says suspiciously: "So what's a trucker doing in Starbucks?"

Mickey says defensively: "Truckers drink coffee, too."

Beth says: "Actually, that really is correct. We get cabbies in, as well, mainly on Mondays."

Jessica says: "I want to meet him."

Mickey says: "In time. First I've got to get this presentation done. Heidelman is coming in from Switzerland next week. This is my big chance. I invited Dad."

Jessica says: "Did he say he'd come?"

Mickey says: "Yeah."

Jessica says: "Gotta go. Lunch with hubby."

Mickey says: "Ciao."

Jessica signs off.

Beth says: "Are you NUTS?"

Mickey says: "There are things you don't know, that I can't tell you, but no, I'm not nuts."

Beth says: "Mickey, you're smarter than this."

Mickey says: "Trust me."

Mickey says, not willing to listen to any more lectures: "Must go."

Beth says: "Meet me for a martini."

Mickey says: "Can't. Got dinner with Dad tonight."

Beth says: "Be careful, Mick."

Mickey says breezily: "Don't worry. I'm going to be fine." And she logged off before Beth could say anything else.

DOMINIC'S CAPTAIN was starting to believe him. The two guys he shot pictures of worked for the labor-union treasury. And that was where he found the connection to Johnny C.

Johnny's brother-in-law had run in an election against one of them. Frankie told Dominic a couple of stories about the campaign. Apparently Johnny C. had pissed a lot of people off, including Vinny.

That afternoon Dominic played pool with Frankie at a ramshackle old warehouse on the South Side. When you asked for a beer, the bartender—he said to call him Willy—pulled a bottle from a freezer full of ice and didn't bother to brush away the chips. The ice-cold liquid was more than tempting, but Dominic just waved it off when Willy offered him a bottle.

A tinny BB King tune played over the speakers, mixing in with the clink of balls and the snap of the bottle caps. Dominic eyed the table and lined up the shot with the nine ball.

"Are you sure that's the one you want?" asked Frankie, just as Dominic was prepared to shoot.

Dom shot him a cold look. "I *was*."

Frankie shook his head.

Dominic straightened and then leaned on his cue. "What?"

Frankie pulled his innocent look. "I just think you're making a mistake."

"And of course you have my best interests at heart. Right?"

"I owe you some favors. I'm trying to be softhearted here. Work with me on this."

"Yeah," Dominic answered, and then bent down to make his shot.

The ball sank sweetly into the pocket. Dominic looked at Frankie, feeling smug and happy.

Frankie bent and lined up his shot. "You could have taken the eleven ball, as well."

"Smart-ass," muttered Dominic, loud enough for Frankie to hear.

While Dominic watched, Frankie sank the five and the two. Then he watched as Frankie sank the one and the four. Sad to say, Frankie sank the eight ball before Dom got another shot.

He handed over a twenty to Frankie. "You're nothing but a hustler."

"And you, my friend, make a fine mark."

Dominic avoided saying anything else. It was already hard enough. He was going to put Frankie away and that didn't sit well. Frankie had a solid heart, even if he did have some basic unlawful tendencies. Dominic knew he was doing the right thing, but sometimes doing the right thing sucked.

"Another game?" said Frankie, his fingers dancing in the air.

"We playing for money?"

"Is there a God?"

Dominic held his hands. "You tapped me all out, big guy."

"You know what your problem is, Dominic? You have no faith in yourself."

"No, I'm a realist," Dominic answered as they walked back to a table in the corner. "Hey, I need you to let me in on Vinny's action."

Frankie leaned back in his chair, hands behind his head. "I'm fresh out of cigarettes."

Dominic held firm under the scrutiny. "I want something bigger. I need a little cash. Michelle's got her eye on a beamer." It was a heavy exaggeration, but in Frankie's current female way of thinking, it would make perfect sense.

"I don't know, Dom. You know I like you and all, but Vinny's such a tightfisted SOB."

"I understand," said Dominic, his fingers drumming on the table. He needed just a little more to push Frankie over the edge. And he knew exactly what that was.

"I could hook you up with Amber. A real date. She can meet Michelle at the park. The four of us. No prying eyes. No listening ears. It can be yours, Frankie. But there's a price."

"I'll do it," said Frankie, falling for it hook, line and sinker.

Even though his superior would approve, it was the second time in his life that Dominic was making deals with the devil.

DOMINIC PUT OFF CALLING Michelle as long as he could. It wasn't that he didn't want to talk to her. It was mainly that the ten Hail Marys he'd said did nothing to alleviate the guilt of bringing her further into his life.

Who was he kidding? She was already a part of his life. Every night they were together, permanence was creeping closer. He could see it in her bathroom shelves. He'd zoomed right past toothbrushes into mouthwash and deodorants. Something about hanging out at Dilly's, and the late-night meetings at the docks made him compulsive about his hygiene. Like minty-fresh breath could erase the feeling of filth.

He picked up his cell phone and dialed.

"Michelle? How's it going?" he asked, as if he hadn't just seen her four hours ago.

"Hey," she said, pitching her voice down low. Intimate. He loved the way she whispered to him when they were together. A soft-spoken wall that kept them from everyone and everything else.

"Let's go to dinner tonight," he said. They didn't do dinner often. His work hours usually ran late, but tonight was quiet. Nobody did business on Tuesday nights.

"I can't," she said. "I've got dinner with my dad."

"Oh," he said, waiting to see if she'd say more. If he were more presentable, she'd be inviting him along. Instead, he was a liability. His rules, he reminded himself.

"I should be back early," she said. "Come over."

He walked into the back room of the warehouse where Vinny was waiting for him. After months of work, things were finally progressing. He was getting in right where he wanted to be. "Ten o'clock?"

"Don't be late or I'll have to start without you."

His mouth went dry, and his cock went right to full liftoff. "Damn, Michelle. I can't go greet the boys like this."

She didn't have any sympathy at all. "You'll think of something," she said, and then hung up.

He put the cell phone neatly in his pocket and his hand searched for the envelope of cash, even though he knew it was there. The fat bulge pressed against his heart. He shoved the doubts away. This was work, he reminded himself. He was doing right. But something felt wrong.

IT WAS TWENTY MINUTES after eight, and Mickey was sitting alone at the best steak house inside the Loop. All around her, men were drinking, smoking cigars and enjoying forkfuls of juicy, medium-rare, prime aged beef. She, on the other hand, had drunk two martinis—dry, eaten half a loaf of pity-bread that the waiter had brought for her and read the colorful history of the restaurant four times.

She'd been stood up. By her own father.

Cursing her genes, she rummaged in her bag until she found her phone and she punched his speed-dial number. Why did she even bother? It takes two to maintain a relationship. *Two.* On the second ring, the efficient assistant, a Mr. Klein, answered.

"Where's my father? I've been waiting for exactly forty-seven minutes in the middle of Chicago, which is more than an hour from my home."

"My apologies, Miss Coleman, but your father cannot be reached."

"Is he in surgery?"

"No."

"Then where is he?"

"He can't be reached," the obstinate man insisted.

She picked up her knife, thinking knifely thoughts. "I'm his daughter."

"Orders are orders," he said.

"What's going on, Klein?"

"Your father is involved."

Finally, the truth. "With what?" she asked.

"A woman."

# 13

TWO ADDITIONAL MARTINIS, one shrimp cocktail and a piece of cheesecake later, the room began to warm nicely. Men glanced her way, and she would wave her fork with a Norma Desmond flourish. Let them stare. The phone rang and she picked it up, sure that her father was calling to apologize.

"Michelle?"

It was Dominic. Even better.

"Hello there, sweet cheeks," she said, smiling at the phone.

"Where are you?"

"Listening to you seduce me. Go ahead. Seduce me."

"Have you been drinking?"

"Is that offensive to you? You know, some men will not touch a girl when she's been drinking. I've never met any of them, though."

"You aren't going to drive, are you?" he said, ever the cop.

She sighed. "You're so cute."

"Don't call me cute."

She giggled. "Cute."

"Where are you?"

"Morton's steak house."

"Don't move. I'll be right there."

"To seduce me?"

"Yeah. Just don't move. And don't drive, will you?"

She kissed into the phone. "Whatever you say, sweet cheeks."

DOMINIC COMMITTED seventeen traffic violations to get to State Street in under ten minutes. It was the longest ten minutes of his life. When he entered the restaurant, there she was, at a table with three sleazy businessman types. Bastards.

Dominic didn't bother with being polite.

He just stood and glowered.

Michelle got up, swaying slightly.

"I thought you were meeting your dad."

She hiccuped. "He stood me up."

His smile was forced, but at least he managed that. Her father was a first-class prick. "Say good-night to your friends."

She waved, a slight wiggle of fingers from a woman who never wiggled her fingers. "Goodbye, boys."

He slapped some money into the maître d's hand. "Thanks for keeping an eye out."

The man sniffed. "You're welcome, sir."

The *sir* made him smile. He loaded Michelle under his arm and half carried her to the car. "You shouldn't drink when you're upset. It's abusing alcohol."

She grabbed his crotch. "You're very sexy when you're giving lectures."

He fought her hands as best as he could, but maybe she copped a feel a couple of times, and maybe he didn't fight quite as much as he would if he were a gentleman.

By the time they made it to Schaumberg, she was passed out. He lifted her in his arms and carried her inside. And after he'd tucked her under the sheets, he removed the glasses and put them on her nightstand.

She looked so different without the thick frames. So soft and vulnerable. Of course, she'd hate it if she heard him say that. He had learned that much about her. He smoothed back the silky brown hair from her forehead. So soft and fine. Gently he kissed her forehead and let himself stare. She didn't like it when he stared, but sometimes he just couldn't help it.

"I love you, Michelle," he whispered, testing the words out where no one else could hear. They felt honest and true. Lying was his native state; the truth just made him nervous.

Then he settled himself in the chair beside her bed, with a bottle of aspirin and a glass of water nearby. She was going to have a mother of a hangover when she woke up.

"So how are you feeling?"

Mickey blinked, then spotted a fuzzy Dominic in the corner. She reached out, grabbed her glasses, and instantly he came into focus.

"I'm feeling good."

"I've got some aspirin for you."

Had she needed aspirin? Mickey looked at him, confused. "Why?"

"You don't have a headache?"

Aha! She remembered—vaguely—last night. "Nope. I have developed a highly utilized tolerance for alcohol." She smiled brightly in case he doubted her.

"You should be careful. Next time you want to go on a bender, you call me instead. You know how many crimes are committed under the influence of alcohol? And if that isn't bad enough, that stuff will just eat up your insides."

Mickey glanced at the clock—8:13 a.m. Way too early for lectures. "I solemnly swear. Cross heart. Word of honor. Next subject."

He took the book off the table next to him and flipped through the pages. "I made plans for Saturday. If you're up for it?"

"Sure."

He looked up, surprised. "Don't you want to hear what it is?"

She shook her head. "Nope. I trust you."

She watched him read through her book, his face intent. Then he put the book aside. Looked at her carefully. A very cop look. "What happened last night?"

"You'll think I'm pitiful."

"Uh, no. You can bet that there's nothing you could do that would make me think that."

"Dad's involved with a woman," she stated and then peered up at him to see how he took the news.

"Is this a new thing for him?" he asked cautiously.

"Oh, absolutely. Dad has, like, zero time for relationships," or so he always told her, "he's married to his job. He's a heart surgeon," she said, because that usually explained everything to people. They'd look at her with awe and reverence because she had sprung from the loins of a heart surgeon. *Yeah, get over it.*

"And he stood you up?"

"He forgot about me," she said, sounding amazingly sad.

Dominic came over and wrapped her up in his arms, exactly what she needed. For some time, she just stayed there, listening to the steady beat of his heart, letting his strength seep into her. It was nice and comforting in a way that martinis could never be.

"I'm sorry," he said, then gently he kissed her.

"It's not your fault," she said with a sniff.

"No, but I don't like to see you in pain."

It sounded so melodramatic, so pathetic when he said that, and she laughed. "I'm fine."

And he knew that was a lie. "Of course you are, but does that mean I can't hold you, or kiss you if I want?"

"You want?"

"I always want."

And he kissed her where it hurt. Right over her heart.

JESSICA SAYS: "Why don't you come over for dinner tonight?"

Mickey says: "Are you cooking? What preternatural event warranted that?"

Jessica says arrogantly: "I'm getting better."

Mickey says, being moderately sarcastic: "I'm sure you are."

Jessica says: "You can bring Dominic."

Mickey says: "AHA! Ulterior motive at work here. I can't anyway. Plans."

Jessica says: "Like what?"

Mickey says: "We're going out with some of his friends."

Jessica says: "Now you just wait one minute. Talk

about your &#*&#% double standard. That is soooooooooo not fair. You can meet his friends, but we can't meet him? I'm sneezing here, Mickey. Can you tell? *I'm sneezing.*"

Mickey hands Jessica a virtual tissue.

Mickey says: "It's something that's important to him."

Jessica says: "And we're not important to you?"

Mickey says: "Of course you are."

Jessica says: "Fine. Go off with all his trucker buddies and just leave us to sit alone and knit."

Mickey says: "You're married. You're not going to knit."

Jessica says: "But I could because I suddenly have all this spare time."

Mickey says: "Good night, Jessica."

Jessica says: "I DON'T LIKE THIS—"

Mickey logs off.

BETWEEN WEDNESDAY and Saturday, Dominic made great strides. He'd reported in twice, pleased with the Captain's praise. Over the past week, a "reliable source" had let a couple of union names slip and now two of the treasurers were going to quietly step down from their posts for getting kickbacks from organized crime guys.

He had taken a bound-for-nowhere case and made it. Or almost made it. The last name was just out of his reach.

There had always been rumors of a corrupt trinity between the Outfit, the union and city council. Vinny had been awfully sure that his construction company would get a piece of the development project down by the old stockyards. Too sure. Dominic would bet his shield that the reason for Vinny's confidence was that the last name of the trinity belonged to an alderman.

Everything was going okay. Well, not quite. The date on Saturday bothered him. Dominic almost called it off. Almost went back on his word. But he needed this case too badly. He had a grand plan. Get Frankie out of the life, get Amber away from Vinny for good and put Vinny away for a long, long time. It was ambitious, above and beyond where the case had begun. Success was starting to taste sweet. Success and something even sweeter. Redemption.

It was the thought of redemption that kept him focused. So on Saturday night, he found himself driving Michelle to Grant Park.

They met up with Frankie and Amber and started out toward the band shell. Frankie, the romantic, had other thoughts.

"Let's go see the fountain."

Dominic rolled his eyes. The fountain was the biggest make-out spot in Chicago. Of course, if he didn't get to make love with Michelle about every night, he'd probably be interested in the fountain, as well. In fact, if he was really paying attention, he should have noticed the way her eyes lit up.

Okay, he was a world-class schmuck.

"You know, I was going to suggest that myself," he said.

They walked across the lawn and Michelle tucked her hand in his. For a minute he could forget this was work. Damn, he should take her out on a regular date.

Something romantic and meaningful, not seedy and fe-
lonious. She was his lifeline. His connection into the
part of the world where he desperately wanted to belong. He wasn't about to let her go.

Amber took off on a fast walk, pulling Frankie behind
her. "I've never seen the fountain at night. It's supposed
to be gorgeous."

Dominic held Michelle back. "Thank you for coming
with me. I owe you big-time for this."

She looked surprised. "You don't owe me for going
out with you."

"Well, it's not exactly a steak dinner at Morton's, and
Frankie, well, he's a little confused in the pursuit of
monetary rewards."

"Can't you forget about work for a little while?" she
said, staring him down from over her glasses.

He blinked twice. Forget his work? He couldn't do
that. The work kept him honest. It was always there,
looking over his shoulder, making sure he did right.
"You make me forget about it," he told her. "And that
can be a dangerous thing."

She looked at him, all serious, her eyebrows pulling
together. "You've got to take care of yourself, okay? No
risks or extra moves. You know when the bad guys start
shooting? You don't jump in front of innocent bystand-
ers, okay? You pull out the biggest gun you have and
shoot."

Dominic smiled at her. "You don't worry about me."
He was never gonna be Clint Eastwood. Clint always
came out on top. Dominic was just happy to stay in the
game.

Quietly they walked over the grass to the giant fountain. The colored lights danced among the brass sea horses, catching the drops in their spell. The pattern changed and the water splashed down, bathed in gold, like tears from an angel.

And heaven decided to laugh at him. He heard the voice first.

"You bitch!"

Vinny was here.

# 14

DOMINIC'S INSTINCTS took over, his walk changing from casual to predatory. He motioned Michelle back, out of the way. Safe. Then he pulled his 9 mm free and tucked it behind his back.

First he'd try the charm and reason route. Directly in front of him, Frankie stood between Amber and Vinny. Vinny had already bypassed the charm and reason route, going directly for the gun.

*Shit.*

Dominic walked up slowly, careful not to startle Vinny in any way. He'd handled a couple of situations before, but Vinny's fuse was short. Too freaking short.

Dominic pulled to the side where he was in Vinny's peripheral vision. *Go with the charm first. Don't blow the case.* "Vinny, you here for the blues? You should head on down to the band shell. Come on, we'll get a beer on the way."

"You're here, too, huh?" asked Vinny, his deadly eyes still pulling a bead on Frankie.

Dominic tried again. "Hell, half of Chicago's here tonight. Amber, come on now, we can go find some supper, or maybe a pizza. You know, Giodorno's got a great pie."

"You need to stay out of domestic disturbances, Dominic."

His hand found the cold steel of his gun. "Ah, Vinny. You know I can't do that. It's the way I was raised. My mom, God bless her soul, was a firm believer in Lancelot or Galahad. I can never get the names straight. She used to whip my butt if I didn't open the damned door for women first. Trust me on this, Vinny, all you need to do is to cool off a little and we'll all be fine," lied Dominic soothingly.

Amber chose that moment to voice her opinion. "I ain't going back with you, you philandering, two-bit goombah. Not tonight. Not ever."

Dominic winced. Not the best way to calm down volatile situations.

Vinny might have been angry, but the gun never moved. The .38 was leveled straight at Frankie. "You been screwing around on me, haven't you, you little slut?"

"And what if I have? You've been delivering more packages than the U.S. Postal Service. What about Stella Roberts? Or Marian West? Do you think I don't hear these things? Do you think people aren't laughing at me?"

Vinny cocked the trigger and pointed it right between Frankie's eyes. "Then there's one less story that nobody's going to hear about."

Dominic edged a half inch closer. "You don't want to do this, Vinny."

"Shut up, Dominic."

Charm wasn't working. Dominic pulled out his gun.

"No, you don't want to do that, Vinny." He placed the barrel against Vinny's head.

Then everything happened fast.

Vinny pulled the trigger.

Boom. Frankie went down, a red rose blooming on his shoulder.

Amber screamed.

Dominic fired.

And Vinny fell to the side, a neat bullet hole in his brain.

Somewhere in the distance, a siren sounded. Low and sad. The cavalry had arrived, but it was too late.

MICKEY STOOD, frozen, not knowing what to do. She couldn't catch her breath. No matter how she tried, air wasn't coming into her lungs. She wanted to run to Dominic, but there was a gun in his hand. And the cops were there, already taking him away.

He looked over at her and his eyes were shot full of pain. At that moment, she got a glimpse of the hell that he lived through. Her own neat, tidy existence was a place where the bad guys didn't use real bullets.

Now, she realized the good guys used real bullets, too.

He looked as if he was going to say something, but she took a step back. It wasn't a big step, but he noticed just the same.

Slowly her body came back to life, her lungs expanding, expanding, her frozen blood starting to warm and pulse. Her brain began to process the images that had transpired.

Yet her feet remained firmly planted on the ground.

The last time she saw Dominic, he was sitting in the back seat of a cop car, staring straight ahead.

Not looking at her at all.

IT CERTAINLY WASN'T the high point of Dominic's career. He was "arrested" and spent twelve hours being processed at Cook County jail. His captain, ticked off at being pulled away from his wife's best meat loaf, had dug him out of jail. It was a bad thing when cops—especially undercover cops—killed a suspect.

The captain put him on leave, pending an investigation. Right now, the investigation into the late Vincent Amarante and the mysterious alderman was closed. End of discussion. And Captain Freeman was headed back home.

"Don't bother me again," were his last words.

Right now Dominic wasn't up to bothering anybody. A man couldn't be any less astute than to miss the shock on Michelle's face. She was scared and rightly so.

He'd always led a life that was more than a little colorful and he always would. That's the way he thought, the way he lived, the way he was.

When Dominic got back to his apartment, he tried to drink a glass of water, but ended up losing it all in the sink.

His first kill.

Silently he made his way into the chair in his living room and turned on the TV, putting the volume up loud, because he didn't want to hear himself think anymore.

Not that it helped. His mind kept pounding away at him anyway.

Dominic had become a cop in order to do the right thing. To protect people. To make it up to his brother.

So what had happened?

Dominic, obsessed with being the hero, the almighty protector of all things frail and fragile, had gotten cocky and careless. He was so sure that things would work out okay. Again.

And somebody had died.

*Again.*

For the last ten years he'd been living in his corner of hell, pretending everything was fine. He'd been wrong.

From the other side of the room, his phone chirped, and he walked over to check the calls. Four from Michelle. He should call her.

*Yeah, honey. Back home from jail. Sorry about the little mishap in the park. These things happen.*

How could he explain his life to her? He couldn't admit the truth to his own father. Somewhere deep inside him, Dominic knew it was time. Coming clean was something that he should have done years ago. In order to start over, he needed to own up to the past.

He started to dial the numbers, playing over the words in his head.

*Dad, I need to tell you something.*

When it came time to punch the final button, he couldn't do it.

He didn't have the courage—not yet.

Maybe not ever.

He threw the damned phone across the room, then sat back down in a chair and let the darkness take over.

MICKEY WAS FRANTIC. No word from Dominic at all. The police had taken her and Amber to the hospital, where they waited for Frankie to come out of surgery.

Amber waited, rocking in the cold plastic seats, her hands clasped together in a tight ball. "He'll be okay," she kept saying, her eyes fixed on the gray doors at the end of the hallway.

"He'll get through it fine," murmured Mickey, trapped in her own thoughts, wondering exactly how much reality the cops would lend to Dominic's cover.

Eventually the doctor came. They were moving Frankie to a room where he would stay for the night. He was going to be fine.

Amber started to cry.

Unable to maintain the rock-hard calm any longer, Mickey escaped to the gift shop, where she bought a pink elephant for Frankie. He'd like that.

Then she checked the battery on her cell, queried her answer machine. No new messages.

The glass shelves were lined with stuffed animals and get-well cards and bright balloons. Then she passed a man carrying a bunch of red roses, the same color as Frankie's blood.

She doubled over, her body giving up to the panic inside her. Hot tears started first. Then real sobs. She needed someone. Dominic.

It seemed so selfish to fall apart. She was just a bystander. She hadn't killed anyone, hadn't been shot at, hadn't watched the man she loved go down.

Yet she hurt. She could still hear the gun blasts echoing in her head. And the god-awful hell in Dominic's eyes. She wanted to hold him, help him survive. But he wasn't here.

The salesgirl was apparently used to customers losing it in the shop. She patted her on the back, telling Mickey that everything would work out.

Mickey started to laugh. Nights like this didn't go away. They got played over and over. Fast-forward. Slow motion. Reverse. Frame by frame.

Eventually the laughter stopped and the tears dried. Now she was a part of his world, and everything that entailed. For better, for worse. Now it was time to deal. Time to grow up. She squared her shoulders, bought two extra balloons from the salesgirl and thanked her for her trouble.

Mickey had always thought that love would be sweet and pretty, full of pink hearts and cute animals that sang in the chorus. It wasn't easy to admit, but she'd been wrong.

THE SUN WAS BLINDING but Dominic squeezed his eyes open. He walked over to the window and stared at the morning light, letting the rays warm his cold skin. Tomorrow had come after all, but he didn't feel any better.

Then he saw the plant.

A dying plant.

*Oh, God.*

No, he wasn't going to let this happen.

So he tried everything. First he watered it until the water pooled at the bottom of the drip tray. Then he fed it with fertilizer. Two scoops, just like the instructions said.

Nothing.

It was hopeless.

Once again, he'd taken something good and ruined it.

Still, he wasn't ready to give up. Not yet. He couldn't give up.

The stupid plant couldn't die.

So he began to talk to it. Talked like Mickey had told him to. What did a guy say to a plant?

"What the hell did she name you?" he started with. "From now on, your name is plant."

The plant didn't answer.

"You know this is pretty stupid, don't you? If it wasn't for her…"

He collapsed into the chair and let his head fall back against the hard, wooden back.

A man could change. Of course a man could change. The problem was, he'd been changing for ten years and he didn't feel any different. He didn't feel any better at all.

*Hell, Dominic, open your eyes.*

The plant sat there, brown, still dying.

It was so easy to just let things slide. Ease back into the same routines. The same lines.

No, this time he could do it.

Then he picked up the phone and dialed.

One ring, two rings. Then his dad answered.

First he did the usual greetings, the usual lies.

"Michelle's doing fine. Yeah, we're still together." *For now.*

"Maybe Christmas." *Maybe never.*

No, he could do this. "Dad, I need to tell you something." *Okay, that part was easy.*

"Sure, I can wait a minute." Dominic clasped the medal around his neck. For courage.

"Everything okay now?"

"It's about Antonio." *I can do this. I have to do this.*

"Remember the summer before he died?"

"Yeah, it was pretty hot that year." He could still remember the way Antonio would pull off his shirt and rub the sweat from his forehead. Just one more thing that Antonio had learned from him.

"Dad?" *I'm not who you think I am, Dad. I don't want you to hate me.*

"Yeah, I miss him, too." *He shouldn't have died. He never should have died. I'm sorry.*

"No, I was just thinking about him."

"I'll definitely be home for Christmas."

"Right now? I'm in Florida. The beaches are great down here. You and Mom would love it."

For thirty minutes he talked to his father, yapping like nothing was wrong, and after he hung up, he took off his medal and draped it over the brown leaves of the plant.

It seemed that some causes were pretty much hopeless after all.

By MONDAY EVENING, Dominic knew it was time. Time to tell her the truth about him and his life. When he knocked on her door, she opened it up and immediately launched into his arms.

Longingly he held her, like he'd never let her go. Once again the consummate liar. He memorized each piece of her, her hair that fell against his cheek, the arms that always clung so tightly and the smell—the sharp, exotic perfume that he'd wake up to every morning for the rest of his life.

Slowly she pulled away.

"Are you okay?"

"Not too bad."

She looked him over head to toe, like she expected bruises or something. "I called and they said you were in jail. You're out now, right? They realized it's all a mistake, right?"

He shrugged, uncomfortable under the scrutiny. "There's not going to be any charges, if that's what you mean. An investigation. Standard procedure."

"Well, of course. I mean, you saved everybody's life. Frankie's, Amber's." Then she started to cry. His strong girl was crying. The sound ripped through him. She pounded her fists against him. "You jerk. I told you not to do anything."

He didn't try to defend himself, just let her hit him, let her work through all the stuff inside her. Besides, he deserved it.

It was some time later when she finally calmed down.

"Feeling better?" he asked.

She sniffed, took off her glasses and wiped her eyes. "I'm fine. Forget what you saw. I'm just hormonal."

It was bull and he knew it, but he wasn't going to argue. "Michelle, we need to talk. Why don't you sit down?"

Instantly her eyes went alert. Maybe it was the words, maybe it was the tone. She walked over to the chair and sat down, her arms folded across her chest. "Sure, go ahead."

He plunged right in. "I need to get my life in order. There's things I need to do, things I need to fix. I need some space for a while."

She blinked. "You need space? You want to call things off, is that what you're saying?"

He didn't want to, but he would if he had to, if he couldn't be the man she deserved. "No," he lied to her, because he didn't think he'd ever be the man she deserved. "I need *time*, Michelle."

"You're just all freaked out because of Saturday. Look at me, I cried. Twice. You can't make big decisions until you calm down."

Dominic's hand went to the chain at his neck, but it was gone. "I can learn to live with what I did on Saturday, but I'm not the sharpest tool when it comes to judgment. I shouldn't have set that up on Saturday, but I wanted the case too badly. I let that get in the way of my brain. Now, this isn't a problem that you have, but me? I'm not any good when it comes to making choices."

Her feet hit the floor and she shot up. "I will not let you trash our relationship just because of one mistake."

He looked around the room, avoiding her eyes. Everywhere there were plants—living, breathing, healthy plants.

How to make her understand? Helplessly he ran a hand through his hair. "That's not the worst of it. It's not one. It's two, or four. God, I've stopped counting them all. You know, when it's just me—when I'm not responsible for anybody else—I do okay. But when somebody depends on me, when I need to look out for somebody, my head gets all weird. Please, sit down."

She sat, her eyes blinking quickly. She was starting to get it. "You're just being hard on yourself," she said quietly.

She thought he was being too hard on himself? God's truth, he had never been hard enough. She still thought he was somebody else. Time to open her eyes and show her what twenty-twenty meant. "I'm going to tell you a story that nobody else in this world has heard. It's not leaving this room. You understand?"

Silently she nodded, and he prepared himself. The words rose inside him, battling with the anger. Penitence won.

He swallowed and started to talk. "When I was seventeen, I wasn't the sterling character you see before you. Most of the guys in my neighborhood weren't. I never got caught. I was always too good. And cautious. Other saps took too many risks. Not me." He glanced up, she was watching him. He couldn't face her, so he turned around and started to pace.

"I had these two brothers. Christopher, he was the baby. No trouble at all. And then there was Antonio. Antonio was the middle brother. He was always trying to fit in. He wanted to be tough like me, but he wasn't. He was sharp like you, but he didn't have my street smarts. Anyway, he wanted to learn to hot-wire cars. Wanted to do some joyriding to show off. I taught him. I showed him every goddamned thing I knew. It took two weeks. For two freaking weeks I played the mentor, thinking this was stuff he should know. Kept him from looking like a wimp, you know? I wanted him to fit in. Like me. So, it was all of two nights later—less than forty-eight hours, that's how long it took—for him to take his very first joyride solo. Unfortunately, a cop spotted him and Antonio ran. He got shot. Antonio Beppe Cordano died in the hospital two days later."

Dominic sank down in the chair across from her and looked at her square-on. He had done right to tell her. To finally confess.

"I've been waiting ten years for someone to condemn me for what I did. I can see it there sitting in your eyes. I kept quiet, because I was scared. I knew I was going to lose everything I had, and I deserved to. I took off for Chicago, not because I was so keen on being an officer of the law. I was just afraid of getting caught."

She sat there, frozen, not giving anything away. Finally, she cut through the icy silence. "Why are you a cop?"

It was an odd question, but he knew the answer. "To make things right. I have to make things right."

"You hate your job?"

"I don't know. I never really thought about it much. It was something I had to do."

"Did you ever think that maybe you were just meant to be a cop?"

"No. And nobody who knew me would think that, either." She was grasping at straws. Not that he didn't understand that, he'd done it, too. "It doesn't matter. I've got things I've got to do. I have to tell my father. I have to fix my screwup with the case."

"You didn't screw up."

"That's your opinion, you're entitled to it. Anyway, it needs to be fixed."

"You'll be back?" she asked.

"I don't know," he said, giving her his best reassuring smile. "Give me time."

He had to come clean with his parents. Fix ten years of lies. He needed to finish the case. Tie up the loose ends of his life. Ends that were starting to unravel on him. He needed to prove to himself that he'd gotten so far entangled in deception that he couldn't find the right way out.

She shot him that arrogant look, but he wasn't fooled. "Don't take too long, Dominic. I won't wait forever. Even for you."

He opened the door, not daring to touch her again. "I know. You remember when you asked me what I was scared of? It's this. I want to be good, I want to do the right things, but I don't know what kind of man I really am. I want to be that man I see when you look at me, Michelle. I have to prove it to myself and to you. But I'm terrified that I'm not that guy. *That's* what I'm afraid of."

Then he closed the door and left.

TUESDAY WAS HELL-DAY. Mickey didn't want to be there, she wanted to be at home. In bed. With her covers pulled tight over her head. But she had the presentation to get ready for.

One more day.

However, she was a Coleman and could shut her emotions down when necessary.

*Right.*

She stayed chained to her desk, pounding at her keyboard. Typing up the last of her notes, wishing she could forget.

She kept on typing, pushing herself until she stopped thinking about him, until she could lose herself in the stars, until she was so tired she couldn't move. Only then did she rise from her chair, stiff and sore. As a reward for actually being productive while suffering from severe depression, she called Beth.

"Where are you?" Mickey asked, noting the background noise.

"I'm with Cassandra at Brick's."

"I'll be over there in half an hour. Save me a seat, huh?"

She didn't bother to change. She wasn't going to meet men, wasn't going to drink herself into oblivion. She was only going to convince herself that all life as she had known it was not completely over.

As she walked in the door, she heard the loud voices, the heavy bass music. So far, so good. Life was carrying on. If all these people were having such a good time, so could she.

Beth and Cassandra had a table in the corner.

"Where's Jessica?" asked Mickey, even though she knew the answer.

"She had to get in bed early tonight," answered Cassandra with an elegant shrug.

Mickey felt that long sword of jealousy rip through her. She thought she'd found her own true love, but no, he had to go find himself.

"How was the dinner on Saturday?" asked Beth.

"Good," lied Mickey, because she couldn't tell them. Somewhere between Saturday and today she had changed. Now she was a little harder, a little stronger, and a lot less dependent on anybody else.

So she smiled a tight smile and everybody bought it.

The waitress came by and asked Mickey what she wanted to drink. She considered all options, thinking that 110-proof oblivion was exactly what she needed, but she had given Dominic her word.

Did she owe him her loyalty?

"Just some tonic water with lime."

Beth raised her eyebrows. "Going a little lightweight, aren't we?"

"I made a promise," said Mickey. And for another two excruciating hours, she suffered through the pain of pretending that everything was fine. That life was wonderful and rosy.

Finally she couldn't do it anymore, so she faked a yawn, talked about the big day she had tomorrow and went home to sleep in her bed. All alone.

On Wednesday, she avoided calling her father. If he showed, great. If not, what did it matter? Although she kept her cell phone set on loud, just in case.

Dr. Heidelman had arrived and was making the rounds, meeting with Dr. Romanowski and then Dr. Meyerson.

Earlier in the day, Dr. Romanowski had brought him by, making the introductions. This was her big moment, and she remembered her manners.

The day dragged on, but finally two o'clock came around. She scanned the huge auditorium, looking for the familiar face of her father. The discreetly balding pate, the stubborn chin, the arrogant eyes just like hers.

He wasn't there.

She decided to wait a few more minutes. Surely he would show. At two-fifteen, Dr. Romanowski hinted that she really needed to start, but then her cell phone vibrated. Caller ID showed UNAVAILABLE.

*About time.* She found a quiet place to take the call, but the only thing she heard was silence.

Frigging technology.

"Hello? Dad, can you hear me? I can't hear anything on your end. Where are you? You're supposed to be here. Remember? Not that I really care or anything... Try and make it, okay?"

Then she hung up. Hopefully he got the message.

DOMINIC LISTENED to the words, not daring to breathe. This was her big moment and she was all alone. He hadn't meant to call, but he wanted to say good luck. Wanted to tell her that he was sorry. Instead, he sat there like a moron, eating up the sound of her voice.

He checked his watch. Not much time left. One quick phone call to the station, and he was on his way.

So far, he hadn't fixed any of his own mistakes, but he sure as hell could fix somebody else's.

THINGS WERE GOING well for Mickey. Nobody had fallen asleep—yet—and Dr. Heidelman looked impressed.

Just when she got to the middle section, the doors in the back opened and her father walked in. She stumbled in midsentence, but recovered.

*About time.*

He went down to the front row and sat. Then he smiled at her, and she felt all of six years old—all over again. Sometimes a girl needed her father. Right now, Mickey didn't have anybody else.

So she focused on talking to him, explaining about the formulas that her team had derived for estimating the density of the different parts of the galaxy. Showed the charts of their work. The more she talked, the more he smiled.

Maybe astrophysics wasn't heart surgery, but it was her love.

She ended up with fifteen minutes for questions and answers, but no hands sprang up. Mickey coughed nervously. Finally, Chao—bless her—raised her hand in the back. Then Heidelman had two questions about the effect of Minkowski on their derivation, and she handled it flawlessly.

All in all, it could have been better, but everyone clapped at the end, including Heidelman. And her father was beaming. She took a little bow, pushed her glasses up on the ridge of her nose and smiled.

She had done good.

DOMINIC EDGED BACK out into the shadows. He shouldn't have stayed, but he wanted to see her. Wanted to hear her use all those big words, and describe concepts that he didn't have a clue about.

She loved what she did. It was there in the glow in her eyes, the vibrancy in her voice. She'd found her dreams. His heart warmed to that. She deserved to find them.

He took one last look at the lab, one last look at the place where the stars came to earth. Then he turned around and headed home. This wasn't where he belonged.

"YOU WERE LATE," Mickey told her father, not wanting it to sound like an accusation but, well, it was. She picked up the last of her notes from the podium.

He had the grace to blush. "I was remiss. Karen wanted me to look at a new couch. I didn't think it would take four hours. What woman takes four hours to buy a couch?"

Mickey decided to tackle the primary issue head-on. "Am I going to meet this Karen? You've been keeping secrets from me, Dad."

He quirked an eyebrow. "I'm not the only one keeping secrets. You didn't tell me you were seeing someone. An officer of the law?"

Mickey blinked. "How did you know?"

"I was nearly arrested this afternoon for not attending my daughter's presentation. I got a long lecture and a rather alarming ride in his car. But I certainly approve."

*Dominic had been here.* "What did he say?"

"Beyond the lecture?"

Mickey nodded, her heart thumping in her chest. *Calm down, don't jump to conclusions.*

"He said that you were friends."

*Friends. The f-word.* But that didn't make sense. "Why did you think we were involved?"

Her father shook his head knowingly, just like Mickey did sometimes when she wanted to show off her superior intellect.

"I'm a heart surgeon, Michelle. Nobody knows the human heart better than I. The man's in love with my daughter. And how can I hold that against him? I love her myself."

Mickey blinked twice, letting the words seep through her. Part of her wanted to hope, part of her knew better, but she was done listening to her heart. *He wanted her?*

He was going to have to prove it. She wasn't about to hurt that way again.

Then her dad threaded her arm through his and they went out to dinner together. They would never have one of the world's greatest father-daughter relationships, they were too much alike. But still, it was a start.

DOMINIC MADE ANOTHER phone call and on Saturday night, he went back to the fountains at Grant Park.

Frankie watched him, his eyes cold. "People will think we're together."

Dominic sniffed. "That's crap. I would never be seen with somebody as butt-ugly as you. I need to tell you something, Frankie. I'm a cop."

And there it was. The truth. Lightning didn't strike him, the world didn't end.

As gambles went, it was a big one, but Dominic was still betting on his instincts, unwise as that might be.

"I knew you were a cop, right at the first moment I laid eyes on you."

The night was warm, and Dominic leaned over the railing, the overspray cooling his face. "No way. No way, man."

"Yup. It's that tight ass of yours. Only cops walk like that."

Dominic shot him a "like hell" look. "You didn't know until I told you."

"Screw you."

For a long time they were silent, but Dominic was there for a reason. "What are you going to do, Frankie? There's evidence. It's not great, but it'll stand up in court."

Frankie watched the water. "You going to testify against me, Dominic the Cop?"

"I don't want to."

"Then you shouldn't."

Maybe at one time Dominic could have cut corners, but not anymore. Now he was testing himself. So far, things were going okay. "I can't do that, either. Do me a favor and I'll do one for you."

"What do you want?"

"Give me the alderman. I want his name. It's the last piece of the case. I'll fix everything else for you. Witness protection. You give the Feds a few cigarette smugglers and an accountant and they'll be ready to kiss your ass."

Frankie laughed. "A pissant alderman? Why is that so important to you? All the politicoes, they're just chump change."

Dominic stuck his hands in his pocket and looked Frankie in the eye. "No, they're not. They're supposed to be doing right, supposed to be representing the good people of Chicago, not taking them. They've got to be punished."

Frankie sighed. "It's Malloy."

"You'll testify to that?"

"Yeah. He took some kickbacks on the highway construction project. Gave it to DeFalco's company for a fee. Now it's your turn. I want a place in Florida. On the beach. And you have to find a job for Amber. Maybe a librarian or something. I bet she's good at that."

"You going to start over?"

"You bet your tight ass."

Dominic held up a warning finger. "Don't be looking

at my ass, Frankie. I don't like it when guys check out my ass."

Frankie rubbed his hands together and laughed. "Dominic, you are such a cop."

*A new life.* It sounded sweet, but Dominic didn't want a new life. He wanted his old one with some minor modifications. "You think guys can really start over?"

When Frankie looked over at Dominic, his eyes held something there. It was hope, and redemption. "I'm betting on it. I found something good. Ain't nobody going to rip it away from me. You know?"

Dominic nodded. "Yeah. I know."

TWO DAYS LATER he called. She had been expecting it—maybe. She'd even practiced keeping her voice calm and subdued, like she was okay with everything.

He wanted to meet her over on the abandoned ball field. She did set one condition. A challenge of sorts. She didn't have him slaying Hydras or stealing golden apples, but it was tough. If he wanted her, he was going to have to work—and work hard.

She pulled out one of her bimbo outfits. The bustier and the miniskirt. Just to let him know what he'd been missing, because she wasn't stupid.

At nine-fifteen she found herself walking—actually struggling to walk in the tall heels—over to the abandoned field. She had made sure she was fifteen minutes late.

Tonight was just like the night she'd fallen in love with him. The early-summer wind blew from the east, the moon was just a silver sliver in the sky and the stars were winking like spilled glitter. It was perfect.

Dominic was sitting on the bleachers waiting for her, more dressed up than usual. Khakis clung to strong thighs and he wore a simple white cotton dress shirt that made his skin look even darker. He smiled when he saw her, and she couldn't pretend anymore. She smiled back. She didn't know what was happening here, but it was good.

"You're late."

She glanced at her watch. "Oh. I didn't notice."

He looked like he didn't believe her, but he let it ride. "You may be wondering why I called."

She hopped up on the bleachers, giving him an eyeful of leg. "Uh-uh-uh. First things first. What's the answer?"

He rolled his eyes and began to recite, "When comparing the ratio of the luminosity emitted in Halpha in relation to the bolometric luminosity for each star, there is almost a constant ratio over the range M0-M9."

*Be still my heart.* She looked at him with new respect. "How did you figure that out?"

He shrugged, his broad shoulders rolling easily. "I called a certain Ms. Chao."

*He was the devil—a kinder, cleverer devil.* "That's cheating."

He grinned, smug and sure. "You didn't specify rules."

"What did you promise her?" she asked, hoping this wasn't going to involve money or sex.

"I didn't promise her anything."

Mickey didn't believe it for a minute. She was learning to recognize the slight dent in the left cheek that appeared when he was exaggerating the truth. Royally, she raised her eyebrow.

"I admit, I might have pried. I asked her how you had been holding up over the past two weeks."

This was going to involve retribution. Chao was going to pay. "What did she say?"

"I gave my word of honor—such as it is—not to say. However, I did say that I thought I knew the cause of your problems, because I'd been having just the same kind. She seemed to accept that, and I also promised that you wouldn't be in before 9:00 a.m. for the next twelve months."

A future commitment, at least for twelve months. It sounded positive. However, appearances could be deceiving. She'd seen a Z-4 quasar turn into a Z-8 just as quick as you please. "What do you want?"

"I want us together."

It was the moment of truth. She wanted to keep her feet planted firmly on the ground. "Why the change of heart?" she asked, the wobble in her voice betraying her.

"I didn't have a change of heart. The heart didn't change, Michelle. It was always there, with you."

She blinked twice. Deep inside her, a glow began, a light brighter and hotter than anything she'd ever found in the sky. His night-dark eyes stayed fixed on her, intent, making promises that she prayed he would keep.

"Did you fix everything?"

He winced. "Most of it. I told my parents."

"Is everything okay?"

For a second he was silent, considering, staring up at

the sky, and then he met her eyes and shrugged. "I don't know. I think so. It's going to be weird for a while. I did the right thing, but it still hurts."

He looked so alone, and she wanted to comfort him, but things weren't right. Not yet. "I'm sorry. You're their son. It'll get better."

"Thanks."

"And what about the job?"

This time he took her hand, his thumb rubbing her palm, a gesture of comfort rather than seduction. "It's going to be hard. I won't kid you. But I need to be a cop. I'm a good one. Maybe I've got my own agenda, but I'm doing right. I know that now. You reminded me of where I stand. Sometimes your head gets a little messed up being undercover. But you're my North Star. I can look up and figure out where I am when I see you."

She inched closer. "You really listened to all that I said?"

"Most of it. You've got to explain a lot to me, though. But I like knowing about the sky and the planets. I like seeing the stars reflected in your eyes."

Mickey considered herself practical and logical and beyond emotional mishmash, but every time he looked at her, she felt a quiver shoot right through her. Irrational, illogical and completely silly. "This all sounds pretty good," she said in a quasi-calm voice.

"You remember the last time we were here?"

"Yeah."

"I didn't get to do what I wanted to." He hopped down and grabbed her by the waist, lifting her to the ground. Then he pointed to the faded wood, the old seat of the bleacher and there she saw it. Carved in wood.

*Dominic Loves Michelle.*

He took her by the shoulders and there was no mistaking the dreams in his eyes. This from a man who didn't believe in dreams. "I love you. It's forever. I don't believe in divorce."

*Oh, my.* Her lips curved in a soft smile. "What are you asking?"

He got down on one knee and brought out a little black box. "Michelle Cushing Coleman, will you marry me?"

"You want to marry me?"

"Only you. I've got to take you back to New York for a week or so. I made a promise. Please say yes."

High in the summer sky, above the heavens and above the stars, a shaft of light shot through the darkness, blazing a trail in its wake. A perfect wishing star for a perfect wish.

And Michelle said yes.

\* \* \* \* \*

THE BACHELORETTE PACT
*continues with...*
*BREAKFAST AT BETHANY'S*
Temptation 975
*Don't miss Beth's story
coming next month—*
May 2004!

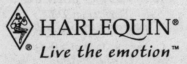

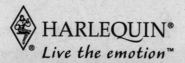

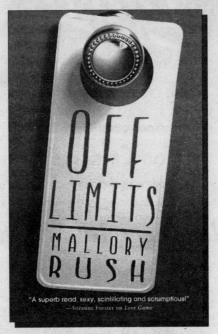
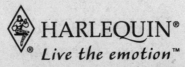

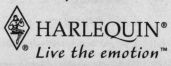

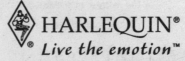